Prologue

Sophora Lilliana deMonstre sat next to her father as the mayor of the town of Villa Morgern explained their plight. She would have been more sympathetic if he hadn't been staring at her like she was edible.

"All of the young women in Villa Morgern have been accosted or torn apart by this beast, and now, it is expanding its domain. Soon, there will be no women of marriageable age in our demesne, and we will be forced to seek our wives in neighbouring towns. Most of my people are not equipped to seek a match elsewhere. They don't have the time."

Sophora watched her father caress his chin in the manner he always did when he was overtaken by greed. Sir Esteban deMonstre was a capable knight and mage, but money was his primary focus. It was why he kept her with him instead of providing a dowry for her. At the age of fifteen, she was prime marriage material.

"What will you offer to me for this quest? My time is valuable."

Sophora didn't look around her at the empty stone halls and walls. All of the money went into magic books and ale.

His lands were extensive, and he was wealthy, but the wealth was in the books he hoarded. There was nothing left for a dowry.

The mayor dropped a bag on the table. "Ten pieces of gold for every troll destroyed."

Esteban picked up the bag and spilled the contents onto the table. "Is this my

Being raised as the Cursed One does things to a person. It changes your relationships and makes you a very paranoid young woman. This is how Sophy ends up in her fourth decade, looking eighteen and having no love life.

The Mage Guild provides her with a liaison so that she can stop calling to rummage through their archives, and the voice in the machines around her becomes an admirable partner, such as he is.

He files a request with her to assist him in his own personal journey, and it takes her into the Guild Hall to face a mage who wants her as a trophy. She isn't impressed, but gets what she needs and gets out of there.

A cursed object that calls to her is part of her plans for the next few days, but the arrival of the body that belongs to the voice throws things into chaos.

Magnus has spent years in amber, waiting to be released by a request from a woman he hasn't slept with. He was born a warrior centuries earlier and is a legendary mage in his own right. He has one major concern, and it involves figuring out the strange pull and repulsion he feels when the Cursed One is around.

Demons, mages, old scores, and cursed objects swirl around the DeMonstre family, and Sophia is first and foremost the Monster Baiter.

The characters and events in this book are fictitious. Any similarity to real persons, living or dead, is coincidental and not intended by the author.

Copyright © 2016 by Viola Grace
ISBN: 978-1-987969-33-7

©Cover art by Carmen Waters

All rights reserved. With the exception of review, the reproduction or utilization of this work in whole or in part in any form by electronic, mechanical or other means, now known or hereafter invented, is forbidden without the express permission of the publisher.

Published by Viola Grace

Look for me online at violagrace.com, Amazon, All Romance Ebooks, Smashwords, Kobo, B&N and other eBook sellers.

Monster Baiter
An Obscure Magic Book 6

By

Viola Grace

retainer?"

"It is."

"You are sure that it is trolls?"

The mayor stopped his leering at her for a moment. "Oh. They are one of the largest gatherings of extranatural beings in the area. We are sure it is trolls."

Esteban swept the coins into the pouch and smiled. "Sophora, prepare to travel."

The mayor licked his lips as he looked at her, and she hid her shiver as she left the room to get the horses ready. This was not going to be a fun trip.

The mayor rode ahead of them, and Sophora said quietly, "Is it wise to go against the trolls? They are not normal monsters. They have villages, communities. They are generally peaceful."

"Sophora, you are my daughter, not my partner. The money offered to me will purchase that Killian manuscript that I have been after. It will complete that portion of my collection."

He glanced over at her and gave her a smug smile. "I am wondering if I draw a knife across your cheek, will it make a difference?"

She knew what he was talking about. He wanted men to stop coming and courting her. They wrecked his study time.

"They are after your money and lands. Either wed and have a son or ignore them. My face isn't even known by any of them. They are usually surprised to see that I am not plain."

He nodded. "You know how I feel about marrying again."

"Yes, it will be a financial burden, and unless a son can be guaranteed, it isn't worth the price." She repeated it as she had dozens of times.

"Correct. Now, we should have kept that unicorn alive. It would add to your mystique when you come with me. Drive up the prices and get the attention of more mages."

Sophora looked away so that he wouldn't see her tears. She had been in love, had felt her heart beat in time with the man courting her, and her father had driven him off before he followed him and killed him. Esteban claimed he was a monster, but she knew that the monster wasn't the man who had brought her roses.

The inn had provided their finest rooms, and Sophora sat by the window embroidering as her father went off to hunt his fourth troll in as many days. His finances were taking an upswing, and he had enough to buy the manuscript.

Two more attacks had happened while they had been in Villa Morgern, and while the girls were not dead, they had been mauled. Sophora used what healing magic she possessed and held their hands while they came back to the world.

A young woman, Melila, whispered, "He knew where I hid. Only my parents know where I hide."

"Describe him for me."

The girl's eyes teared. "He was huge. Larger than any man in the village. There were giant fangs, shreds of fabric on him, and his claws and... between his legs..."

"Whatever you feel comfortable telling me." Sophora held her hand and kept her expression calm.

"The shouting stopped him from doing more than cutting my clothing away and clawing me. He was going to..."

Melila was sixteen and engaged to the baker. Her family was devastated that he might change his mind.

"I will make sure that they know

nothing happened. I will swear by my blood."

Melila's eyes filled with fat tears of gratitude.

Sophora spent time with her and the other girl, Kimsa. When she was certain that the girls would physically recover, she left the room.

"Melila was not defiled by the beast, though that was his intent. Who else knew about the hiding place in your home?"

She listened as they spoke, and her father came home with another troll head.

She had to tell him before he went out again, but he would not listen to her until he bathed and rested. It was frustrating beyond belief.

The next morning at breakfast, she told him. "Father, it isn't the trolls."

He blinked and smiled. "Of course it

is, Sophora. I have the money to prove it."

"No. The creature is inside the town walls. It knows them. It is a member of the community."

He tore off a chunk of bread with his hands and slathered butter on it. "How did you come to this conclusion?"

"I talked to the survivors. One mentioned a gold medallion on his chest. It has power."

"You know this because..."

"I scryed for it. I looked for an enchanted signature, and it was moving in daylight, within the walls. I couldn't pinpoint who it was on, but the magic is here, and it is close."

Her father got to his feet and wove his hand through her hair, pulling her head back. "I have told you what I think of you casting spells."

"Yes, Father." Appealing to their relationship was all that she had. Defensive spells had been completely forbidden.

He pulled out his knife and cut into her cheek. She met his gaze as he drew the line in blood. Fire burned along her skin until her magic flared up and sealed the mark.

"You can't help yourself."

"I am my mother's daughter. She was an immortal until she married you. Troll bride, to be precise. You didn't look behind her then, and you will not see what is in front of you now. If you want proof that the beast is in the city, I will be bait."

He let go of her hair and stepped back. "Clean off the blood. What do you mean you will be bait?"

"I will draw the monster out so you can see it. I will take it out of the town and into a place where it can safely be dispatched."

"You expect me to follow your asinine plan? You are a girl; what do you know?"

"I know that girls like me are the ones targeted and defiled, if not killed. He will seek me because I will be easy prey. You have never turned down an easy hunt in your life."

He mulled it over for most of the day but finally said, "I will follow you from a safe distance. You had better be right."

She knew what he would do to her if she were wrong. She bore the scars from the days of learning what it meant to waste her father's time.

Her body couldn't heal something inflicted with enchantment. The scars he had given her had been something he wanted her to remember.

She was putting her life on the line for this village, and they would never even know.

Sophora walked through the village at night. She had put it about that she had to go out and gather night-blooming herbs. Anyone who had heard about it would know where she was going to be.

She had her basket, tools and a few more items in her possession as she walked through the town before she left the gates and entered the forest.

She knew where she was going to lead the beast behind her. She could feel his focus on her as she headed through the paths and over the roots. She twisted and turned her path, making him fight to keep up with her.

His stumbling and eager growls told her how much he was enjoying the hunt. If he caught her, she would be shredded in no time.

She finally made it to the clearing that she sought, and she reached into her basket, throwing a circle of salt around her and waiting.

He lumbered into her field of vision as the last grain of salt fell.

She had been forbidden defensive

magic, but this was a charm.

The creature was larger and meaner than the ladies had described. Matted hair streaked with blood clumped on his body, his erection was large, and his hands were enormous. He would tear her to pieces if she were lucky.

The beast had a golden charm in its chest, nearly lost in the fur.

Her father crept up behind it and lifted his sword. A moment later, a head rolled across the ground, and it turned back into the image of the mayor.

Sophora wiped the blood spray from her face, and she looked at her father. "He was the cause. Those lives you took were for nothing."

"Not for nothing. They were for gold. Well, you were right. We can go home now." He wiped off his sword, picked up the head of the mayor and left the body with the gold medallion embedded in the chest.

She quickly knelt next to the body and dug the charm out of the skin. It had been bonding and would have become permanent after some time. How many lives would it have taken?

She tucked the charm into her basket and followed her father, getting things together and leaving the town, telling the locals that the beast would trouble them no more.

They rode out, and the sky dimmed. The path that was clear a moment earlier was washed out in an instant. They were forced into ever-smaller paths until they ended up at a village.

Sophora sat on the horse and waited while her father looked around. His horse spooked and threw him. He landed on the ground in a clatter of armour and gold coins.

Sophora's mare was perfectly calm.

Invisible hands gripped her father and pulled him forward into a large circle of polished earth.

"Sophora, help me!"

She had never felt more helpless in her life. "I have no magic that would help you. You need defensive magic, Father."

She watched as trolls surrounded him, keeping him in the centre of the circle, but then, other species appeared. Elves, brownies, a werewolf, a vampire. They gathered and surrounded her father, chanting and whispering.

A troll bride walked to Sophora. "He is being cursed by those he called monster. What do you think?"

She smiled weakly at the beauty in front of her, knowing that the wrong answer would end in death. "I think that he needs any clarity you can provide."

"Excellent, niece. He is being given the ability to see monsters truly so that he will know what to kill."

Sophora inclined her head. "Thank

you, Auntie."

"For you, you saw the monster but did not know what to do, so through his blood, we curse you to see what needs to be done, and you will have the magic to do it."

Esteban was screaming as the magic nested in him before blooming.

"His blood, Auntie?"

"Do not worry, child. We will not kill him."

The troll bride stood next to Sophora, her face and body from the front beautiful to behold, and the back of her a mass of tangled twigs and branches. Her calm in the face of Esteban's agony had a deep satisfaction to it.

Her mother had been such a woman. Esteban had taken her for her magic and the money of her family's territories. She left when Sophora was five. No longer could she be a wife to a man who saw her as a monster.

When he was exhausted and the magic users had parted ways, Sophora got off her horse, found his and helped her father back into the saddle. The magical creatures in the woods watched her as she helped her father straighten up, but they made no move to stop her.

She led him toward home. Two days after they had left the troll village, they stopped by a calm stream, and Esteban saw his own reflection. She had no chance to speak when he lifted his dagger to his neck and cut his own throat.

His whispered gurgle was his last word. "Monster."

Sophora used the money to buy the Killian manuscript, and when the previous owner delivered it, she smiled at the half-elven mage, and he smiled back. She saw no monsters in his eyes.

They were married in the spring, and she began to tour in search of true monsters after her first-born daughter was in her arms.

Sapphire deMonstre was the next line of monster hunters. It was in her blood.

Chapter One

Sophia sighed and put her hands on her hips. Her car was steaming and billowing something that was nearly smoke but mostly vapour.

She flipped her blonde hair over her shoulder and stomped her foot. "Dammit!"

She heard the low growl from the forest surrounding the road and carefully bent low over the engine, wiggling her butt in the air. The skirt flipped around and ruffled in the evening breeze.

"I guess I am going to have to call a tow." She stood straight and sashayed around to the passenger side of the car, opening the passenger door.

She bent forward, and the growl sounded again; arms gripped her, hauling her back into the woods.

She screamed long and loud, a blood-curdling shriek that made her captor press his hand over her mouth, smothering her until she passed out.

Her last thought was that phase one was complete.

She woke, tied to a bed, in what appeared to be a basement or bomb shelter. The smell of concrete was strong.

"You aren't from around here." The beast growled at her.

She took in the aspects of his appearance, breaking down the possible origins of each of the components. Her eyes flicked closed, and when she opened them, she could see the glow of emotional magic.

Of course. This was a spell of insecurity. Fear cascaded into power, and the result was standing in front of her.

She struggled to sit up, but she was firmly fastened to a pipe as well as the base of the bed. She grunted. She needed to find the charm that was turning him from human into the beast in front of her.

Sophia looked at the creature and tried to put on a mask of fear. She let herself think of visiting her great aunt on the weekend, and the scent of fear filled the air.

He nodded, and a vicious grin filled his features, exposing the tusk-like lower teeth.

"You are in my power. What school do you go to? I don't recognize the uniform." His voice was garbled because of the teeth, but he had had enough time to practice his speech.

It would be hard to threaten a woman if he couldn't speak to her.

"Gunning College. I was in town looking to transfer, and my car exploded."

He grinned and stepped toward her. "Lucky me."

She leaned back. "What are you? You aren't any extranatural I have ever seen before."

He chuckled and glanced toward a horn on a shelf. Of course. It was usually a horn that got their attention.

She focused on the object as he approached her, and the light wrapped around the horn, lifting it and snapping it to her fingers.

She held it, and while he lunged for her, she muttered in mage languages until she felt the horn unlock. The magic unravelled, and the beast became a man again.

Well, man was a bit of an overstatement. The boy in front of her was a lean seventeen if he was a day. He was also very naked.

Sophia held onto the horn and

snapped the binding on her wrists and jerked her legs free. The lad was shocked.

"What... how..." The brunette looked down and ran for a set of sweatpants.

Sophia fished her phone out of her cleavage and made a call. "Captain Miskin? I have the highway stalker in my custody, he has been neutralized, and I am asking you to trace my phone and come and collect him."

"*Who am I talking to?*"

"Sophia DeMonstre."

She could almost hear him sitting up on the other end of the line. "Trace is happening and we are on our way."

She left the line open and faced the kidnapper.

The teen slumped on a chair, and he was still wondering what had happened. "I don't understand."

"Which part? You grabbing the horn and unleashing your rage or turning back into yourself? Pick one and I will explain it."

Sophia cocked her head and nodded to his clothing. "Get dressed. I will wait."

He swallowed. "You said you were in college."

"Yes."

"How old are you? You talk a lot older."

He got up and pulled on his sweatshirt and sneakers.

She grinned. "Oh, you don't need to know that. Imagine that I am the same age I look. It will make you feel better."

They sat in silence until they heard the approach of the officers.

"Who is coming for me?"

"Mage Guild. The officers will take you into custody and charge you with misuse of magic. The horn has been made useless, and once it is used in your investigation, it will be destroyed."

He jolted. "You can't."

"Oh. I can. In fact, I am one of the only ones who can." She walked him out to the mages, and they took over. The looks she got in her cheerleader outfit were close to leers, but when she pinned them with her gaze, they looked respectfully away.

She put the horn in an evidence case and took their card so she could fill out the report and send it to them in the morning.

"Ms. DeMonstre, is that your car in the road?"

"Yup." She walked with them back to the highway with a spring in her step.

"Can we help you get it started?"

Sophia chortled and walked to her hood, removing the support rod and lowering it with a click. She tapped the hood twice, and the car roared to life.

"I have it under control, Officers, but thanks for the offer." She climbed into her car, waved them goodnight and headed back to the office in Redbird City. She really hated commuting, but when humans became monsters, she was the DeMonstre on duty.

Her parents looked at her and laughed. Her father grinned. "The cheerleader again?"

"It rarely fails and has a wide age range for attractions. Thanks to this curse of ours, I won't ever look my age, so why not?" She walked through the entryway and toward her change room. The sheer amount of fantasy costumes that she had sometimes embarrassed her, but the weird part was that she could wear the same ones her mother had, and her mom wasn't born a DeMonstre.

While the family name was passed from daughter to daughter, her father, Gerard, was the rare DeMonstre male. He still looked to be twenty-five, and his elegant demeanour gave him a European flare.

She grabbed some normal clothing and stepped behind the changing screen. Her instinct was confirmed a moment later when her parents knocked on her door.

"Come in." She pried the top off and slipped her comfy shirt over her torso.

"How did it go, Sophy?"

"It went fine, Dad. It was a little bit of *oh no my car broke down* followed by *whatever will I do* and a lot of waving my ass in the air, but he took the bait."

Her father was eager. "What was the enchantment?"

"It was a simple rage-to-animal focus. The guy was definitely socially awkward and desperate for female attention. The manifestation was boar, bear, a touch of wolf and some fox. The trigger was a standard cow horn that would have had no place in the forest. It would have

stood out to even the blindest of seek-
ers."

"What about his lair?"

"Bomb shelter under a cottage in the
woods."

Gerard made a frustrated growl.

"Relax, Dad. I know that if you could
be out there, you would be. There just
aren't as many female monsters seeking
men as there used to be. Don't worry.
You still look pretty."

Her mother chimed in. "I keep telling
him that he should take up acting or, at
least, running around naked, but he re-
fuses. He misses being the Cursed One."

Sophy finished smoothing her tights
and tucking them into her knee-high
boots. Her tunic fell to her knees and
was slit up her thighs. She wrapped a
wide belt around her waist and fluffed
her hair out.

The cheerleader outfit went back on a
hangar, and if she didn't have to wear it

for another decade, she would be fine.

She brought it out and added it to her costume library.

Her mother had brought in a tray with coffee and sandwiches. Soph sighed and sat at the small table and broke down the details of her evening.

"How did the car enchantment work?"

"Like a dream, Dad. There was smoke, noise and the scent of overheated metal. It worked like a charm."

"Any idea how the charm found the monster to begin with?"

"Tracking spell to find an angry and disgruntled teenaged boy who wants to get laid is like shooting fish in a barrel." Sophy leaned in and loaded a pile of teeny sandwiches onto a plate.

She sat back in her chair with one foot on the edge and stuffed her face.

Her mother took out a notepad and started to create the statement. "Which

Mage Guild were you dealing with, dear?"

"Creath Township. Captain Miskin. He was there for the arrest."

Her father gave her a calm look. "What do you think his sentence will be?"

Sophy mumbled around some sliced ham and cucumber, "It will be light. He didn't actually do more than chase the first few girls. If I hadn't come along, it would have been different, but as it is, his life may be fairly normal."

Her father nodded. "Of course. No blood."

It was amusing that he liked to reiterate what all DeMonstre's knew. Blood locked the monsters. The more kills, the harder it was to break the enchantment without killing the charmed one. Sophy could still do it, but her target rarely survived.

Her mom got down to it and got the

details from original call-out information to the names of the officers who took the horn into custody.

When her mom was done, Sophy just signed the document and smiled. "I am going to head home if you don't mind."

Her mother smiled and said. "One more cup of tea. You look pale, Soph."

Sophy sat and drank another cup of the medicinal tea. When she was done, she left the family home and headed down the street to her small house.

Living away from home had been vitally important to her. With her features looking eternally youthful, it was imperative that she did things that suited her age. She had bought the house in her early twenties and had paid it off as soon as she could with her own funds.

Acting as a curse breaker didn't pay the bills. She was an accountant, just as her mother and father were. Together, they managed a small empire of financial information.

She had work to do in the morning. It was tax season.

She opened her door with a small flick of magic and walked inside, locking the door behind her.

It felt so good to be in her own territory where every inch of the space gave off energy that she could read, touch and control.

She poured herself a glass of wine and went to run a bath. On the edge of her tub was a single glittering scale. "Delwin!"

Her roommate stumbled out of bed, and she heard him tracking his way to the bathroom. "Oh, you are home. How was the forest perv?"

"About how you would think. What did I say about you using my tub? There is a perfectly good tub in your en suite. Leave mine alone."

She flicked his scale at him. He

caught it and sighed. "I thought I got them all."

"You didn't. Is there a reason that you keep sticking yourself into my personal space?" She scowled at him.

He shrugged; his dark hair over his shoulder and his green-casted skin had a rich tone that meant he was blushing. "Your tub is bigger. I can stretch out my tail."

She smacked him on the shoulder. "Then get your own place and you can have it all."

He sighed. "I can't afford one."

"Get a job. I am really not in the mood to come home to an empty fridge and scales in my tub after every mission. I need controlled space where there aren't any other energy patterns in the vicinity to come down."

He blinked both sets of lids. "Sorry. Didn't think of it that way."

"Please do. You have been here for

four months, ever since that freaking necklace backfired. Get on with your life in the deep and enjoy yourself."

Delwin pouted. He did it very well. "I like it on land."

"I am sure you do. There is probably another extranatural or human out there who would love to take you on and care for you. I have a life, as weird as it is."

He smiled. "I know. It gives me plenty of time to research this realm."

The shark-like, pointed teeth didn't even make her flinch.

He couldn't open her spell books. He had tried several times. They shocked him with huge arcs of power.

She had gone to the store, brought in a mer-to-English dictionary and a huge stack of history books and magazines.

He had spent his days reading and learning about the modern world. When he was done with that, she had given him a clothing allowance and sent him out on his own.

He had found every bar that catered to adventurous sexuality and located his particular niche. His niche involved a lot of glitter and very good-looking men who could hold their own with a merman out of water.

"I think you need to stop with the research and jump in with both feet. Somewhere else."

"I think we get on well as roommates."

She winced. "I never wanted a roommate. I wanted you to learn to speak the language so you would feel more at home. I didn't mean *my* home!"

She started to strip while he stood there. He quickly left her alone.

Sophy washed out the tub before adding bubble bath and watching it churn into a white, gleaming froth that she slid into with a happy sigh.

"Fuck." She grimaced at the glass of

wine that she had left on the bathroom counter. She wasn't a fan of domestic magic, but it turns out she didn't need it.

"I brought you some brownies, and here is your wine." Delwin set the wine on the wide edge of the tub and placed the small plate of brownies next to them.

"You baked?"

He smiled. "No, one of my new beaus is a pastry chef. When I told him you were an accountant, he got all sympathetic about your current stress level. He sent these along. I only ate two." He winked.

She sighed. "Thank you. I appreciate the gesture, but I stand by my statement. You need to get out on your own."

He crouched next to the tub. "I know. This world is just so full of everything. The ocean is huge, vast and wide expanses between communities. Here, I feel lost in a sea of living beings. It is enough to make me scared on a daily basis. I like living with you. It gives me a sheltered alcove from the storm of the city."

She wrinkled her nose. "Fine. Pay rent, get a job and stay out of my tub. If you are good, I will get you a soaker of your own. This deal changes if you are caught in my territory again. If I have to put up a ward against you for my private space, I will."

He grinned again. "Thank you. You won't regret it."

She snagged a brownie, held her wine and sank back into the hot water and bubbles. "I probably will. Out!"

He leaned forward, kissed her cheek and left her alone.

Sophia nibbled at the brownie and sipped at her wine. It seemed that when exhausted and confronted with chocolate, she was a pushover. At least he did the housekeeping.

Chapter Two

Sophia was into her fourth return of the day when she got a call.

"Is this the Cursed One?"

She winced at the name but answered. "Yes. At your service."

"I have need of your services. My name is Lerovan Assingar, and we have a situation with some rogue minotaur in our area."

"Sir, I think you would need to call the XIA for that. I only do curses."

"One of them has gone insane. I don't want him injured." The older man's voice wavered. "They are my sons."

She silently cursed. "The XIA is a better bet."

"It was only supposed to be one of them. They weren't supposed to change together."

She knew thirty-four extranatural languages, and each one was chanting *shit* in her mind. "Give me your address."

"Durban road, the house with the red roof near Morrigan Way."

She nodded as she jotted it down. "I can be there in an hour."

"Thank you so much."

Sophia organized the return she was working on, clipped all categories together and walked over to her father's office.

He saw her face and sighed. "You got a call?"

"I did."

"Dangerous?"

"I have no idea until I get there. You know the drill."

He sighed. "Yeah. Times like this I

wish I was born a girl."

Sophy grinned. "That is just because you want to drop the work and go running through the woods in search of monsters."

"Definitely. Have you gotten the file in order?"

"Yup. Just ready for final entry. The file has been transferred to your computer."

"Thanks. Have fun and keep us posted if you need any help. We will do what we can."

She smiled and made sure that he had everything before she left. In the car, she brought up myths and legends on her audio system, and on the way, she learned all she could about minotaur.

The minotaur were beasts, well, one beast in particular. They weren't a species; they were a demigod. One horny queen was cursed, and the form of the curse was her lust for the sacred bull that her husband refused to sacrifice. The end result was the minotaur.

Every seven years, seven Athenian youths and seven maidens were sent as tribute, and they were dumped into the labyrinth to try and run for their lives. None of them escaped, but it seemed that at least one woman of the final batch managed to come out of it with a child. The curse continued.

She kept driving and asked, "Cross-reference shifter archives."

"Minotaur is not available in shifter archives."

"Mage archives."

"Not available in mage archives."

Sophia bit her lip. "Reference minotaur in mythical archive."

"Result. Minotaur, family name Assingar. Curse transfers to eldest son on his twenty-fifth birthday. See also, god curses."

She made a face at her research computer.

"I saw that, Sophia."

"Apologies, Magnus."

"Accepted." Her computer hummed happily.

Having an intelligent computer had been a great idea, but having a soul bonded to it was a bit of a surprise. She was used to him now, but Magnus was a tricky customer that wanted her to show appreciation now and then.

He was embedded into her computer system, and she could access him from any monitor anywhere. He followed her like a puppy. He also stalled her car on command. It was handy when stalking cursed humans.

He wasn't the same as Benny's Pooky, but it got the job done.

She smiled slightly as the thought reminded her of the unusual wedding that she had bought a one-time-only dress for. Benny's quad union was unusual, but it had been well worth the cost of the outfit.

Out of all the friends that she had thought might end up in a poly union, Benny hadn't even made it into the top twenty. Demon spawn or not, she was just a little on the quiet side.

Sophy sighed and thought about her own options.

"Why the sigh, Sophy?"

"Just thinking about my lack of a love life. When my dad was my age, I was five. It is weird to think that my time should be running out."

"Do the Cursed Ones go through early menopause?" Magnus's voice was dry.

"Funny. No. Not that I know of. We look the same until we die, stuck forever with youth and beauty. Or so I am told."

"You are very beautiful."

"I am the combination of my parents' genes. But, thank you."

"If I was still around, I would be

courting you this minute."

She blinked. That was the first time he had made any kind of flirting reference. "How long have you been dead? Courting dates you in the previous century."

"I met your great, great grandmother shortly before I was taken."

"Taken?"

"Yes, I disobeyed guild rules, and this was my punishment."

She made a face. "What did you do?"

"A conversation for another day. You are at your destination."

Sophy blinked. "Oh. Right."

She had nearly forgotten why she was there. With a low hum, she pulled into the driveway and rolled up toward the house.

The house was huge. Bull heads adorned all of the fence posts, were mounted on the garage and over the door. It was the right place.

When she left the car and headed for the house, the door opened and a huge man with dark hair walked toward her. Streaks of grey peppered his hair.

He paused. "Are you the assistant?"

She chuckled and extended her hand. "I am Sophia DeMonstre. The Cursed One."

He took her small hand in his calloused grip, and she could feel him looking for power. She gave it to him.

He flinched and stepped back as the magic that clung to his body was stripped away from him at her whim. It was a fun trick that would last about an hour.

"What did you do?"

"I just proved who I was, Mr. Assingar. Now, tell me about what happened."

He nodded and beckoned her to come inside. The house smelled of wood and the outdoors. Elemental earth magic was definitely in play in his family. It didn't come from the male side, so perhaps, it was the mother of the children that made the difference.

"Where is your wife?"

He paused in the act of getting some lemonade out of the fridge. "She died when they were born. It is a common side effect of breeding with my family."

"Do you have a family tree I can look at?"

He frowned. "I have an old family bible."

She blinked. "May I see it?"

He nodded and left her alone with the lemonade while he disappeared into the recesses of his home.

She looked around at the pictures on the wall. It was he and his wife. Him and his two boys as babies, and then, the two boys together and one portion of the curse made sense. The boys were twins.

Twins were magical dynamite. One

never knew when their link would blow the connection all to hell. With a family curse, the complications would be mindboggling.

Lerovan returned, and she hadn't had any of the lemonade. He frowned. "You aren't thirsty?"

She smiled and sipped without ingesting any of the liquid. It was a skill that she practiced over the course of years. A lot of the monsters liked to use drugs.

He smiled. "Right. So, here is the family bible. My sons were the last entry."

She looked from the names of Dolin and Borik born to Jessica Yorful Assingar. Yorful. *Oh darn.*

She fished out her phone and kept the volume down so that Magnus wouldn't ask questions. She looked up the Mage Guild records and the Yorful bloodline. Yup. It was a family trait of split souls.

"Your wife was one of twins?"

He nodded. "Her twin died when she was a child. There was an accident."

"Right. Not so accidental." She pinched the bridge of her nose.

"What? Jessie always said it was an accident."

"They always look like accidents. They aren't accidents. Oh geez."

Lerovan scowled. "What are you talking about?"

"Your boys are hostile toward each other?"

"Yes. Boys will be boys."

"No, it is the same boy in two bodies. Normally, he would have killed the extra body by now. The homicide usually happens in childhood."

"I don't understand."

She turned her phone to him and showed him. "You see this? This is the bloodline. It goes straight from either boy or girl. Only one child survives to adulthood, and the other is buried.”

“No. My boys will work this out.”

Sophy cocked her head at him. “If you thought so, why did you call me?”

He smiled suddenly, and it wasn’t a polite smile. “I needed to lure them in, and you are only bait that would come to me. The sedative should be kicking in shortly.”

She blinked at the lemonade and gave him a bland look. “I have no trouble being bait, but drugging me doesn’t work.”

He frowned. “You drank it. I saw it.”

Sophy shrugged. “I am going to get my gear and head into the woods.”

“You will not hurt them.”

“Of course not. I am going to lure them in to let them hurt each other. One needs to die. It is the family trait. You can’t change it. They will go mad if they continue aging, and then, the XIA will be at your door. You will lose both bodies, not just one.”

She got to her feet and headed to the door. He spun her around, and she saw his fist coming toward her. She ducked and drove her fist into his crotch with as much force as she could muster. She was pretty sure she crushed something under her knuckles.

With a deep sigh, she shook her hand out and left the house.

Sophy didn't like what was going to happen next, but it was necessary for the safety of those in the area.

The trunk of her car opened as she approached, and she looked at the array of weapons and fabric. She stripped and changed into some wide-legged, loose trousers with a huge belt. Her torso was bare, with nothing but glyphs and markings painted on her skin. Her hair was back in a ponytail, and she was barefoot.

She called medics for Lerovan, warning them that they needed two vehicles, but one was going to be needed in less than an hour.

She took her long blades and strapped a dagger to one hip as she walked into the woods. She was perfectly content to be bait, but it was going to be on her terms.

Chapter Three

Her first step into the woods snapped her into the enchantment. The words *welcome to the labyrinth* should have been printed on the trees.

The curse that made them minotaur wrapped the miles that surrounded them. Anyone foolish enough to get close would be trapped.

She walked into the woods and followed the path that her senses gave her. The quick change into semi-priestess garb would make them pause, but it wouldn't stop them.

The glyphs on her arms tingled and warned her that he—or they—were near.

She looked around for a nearby rock,

anything to get her a better vantage point. It took a few wrong turns, but she managed to get herself onto a wide, flat piece of granite. She knelt and chanted, calling to them, bringing them in.

The bellow in the woods made her tense, but she kept chanting. The spells that she needed were long and drawn out. Calling on the old gods was always a bit of a gamble. Pointing out a mistake in a long-standing curse was deadly dangerous.

The first blast of air from the first one's lungs was soft. He was looking at her. She kept chanting, explaining her need.

She heard his feet crushing the blades of grass behind her, and she listened for another set of footfalls. His brother was quieter. She only heard a soft rustle in the shrubs as his sibling walked around her, sniffing and snuffling until he circled in front of her.

Sophia had seen scarier monsters but few had had the intense look of fascination in their eyes that the bull-headed man had as he stared at her.

His nudity wasn't a surprise. His father had wide shoulders, a hugely developed chest and still a narrow waist. His son was nearly done becoming a man, but the animal nature was definitely in full control. The lust that was riding him was also evident, but she was able to ignore that by concentrating on the sounds instead of the images.

She whispered chants, waiting for the response of energy, no matter how faint. When the second bull head appeared and the brother joined his sibling, things were coming to a head.

They eyed each other warily, walking around her, keeping her between them.

When one would step toward her, the other would snort, and she continued her work.

Hours passed as she continued to ask for what she needed. A trickle of power finally came to her and told her what it needed. Thankfully, it was the same thing she had planned.

She set down all weapons but her dagger and rose to her feet, stepping into the glade and allowing the minotaur to get closer.

Sophy stood quietly and let the beast men come. They circled her for several minutes before the one on her left made his move. He grabbed at her arm and pulled her against his chest.

She screamed as she was supposed to and let the events unfold.

The other beast bellowed a disagreement, and he grabbed her arm, pulling her away from his brother. Sophy was slammed into the chest of the second minotaur and then pulled away. The fight for the tribute was on.

She backed away until the rock was

pressed against her bare spine and shoulders.

The bulls now had their cow to fight over, so they fought.

Calls, snorts and, finally, the collision of head against head, horns scraping horns and finally goring flesh.

Sophy watched what she had set in motion. The thud and impact of skin on skin made her flinch. Knowing that she would have been helpless in the grip of just one of them, and now goading two into a death match, she felt a curl of nervousness roll up her spine.

The smell of blood filled the air as sunset threatened, and their horns did their work as they collided over and over again.

When the left brother fell to the ground, blood shooting from his muzzle, she left her safe place and walked onto the crimson battlefield. Her bare feet squished in the blood.

She knelt at his side and continued chanting.

In her words, she told Neptune that his bull had been sacrificed, and he was free to remove the curse. There would still be a minotaur to carry on the mythos, but he could pull the power from this one man.

A trickle of energy ran through her, and she touched the minotaur's elbow. It was one of the only spots not scratched or bruised.

The power unlocked the minotaur energy, and he reverted to human. His brother thickened up and gained the power that had been lacking.

The man next to her rolled over, blood burbling from his lips. "Who are you?"

"I am the one to walk you into your death."

"I don't want to die."

"Your body has to give up its soul.

Your brother needs it to keep control."

She took his hand and held it as his breathing slowed.

She heard the thick whisper, "If he needs it, he can have it."

The last exhalation was done with a smile, and he dropped to the ground.

Sophy muttered, "Come on, come on."

The soul freed itself from his body, and she redirected it to the minotaur. The bull man roared as he was made whole.

She ignored him. She had to go to work.

The Cursed One only took over when she was an adult, because every moment of every day since she could walk was spent learning spells, hexes and chants until she was more magic than living being.

Calling a soul was not an easy task. She had to find one and pour the energy down into the body, letting the cellular memories take over and rule. Finding a blank soul was tricky, but that was why she was wearing the glyphs.

She triggered the markings on her arms and raised them up, calling a new soul that hadn't made a mark on the world. It took ten minutes, but a bright strand came to her, wrapped around her fingers and she took it, holding it to the lips of the dead man.

He started to breathe, and she wrapped him in healing magic, lifting him from the ground and holding him safe as the soul bonded to his body and the injuries sealed and healed.

"Can I help?"

She looked over her shoulder, and the man next to her was the dead ringer for the one in front of her, but he was healthier.

"Drop the labyrinth so the medics can get in. They have been crawling around the edges for hours.”

She watched as the cleared twin slowly opened his eyes as he floated. “Bor, what the fuck is going on?”

“You get to finish your doctorate, Del. Just stay still while she works on you.”

Dolin looked to her, and his eyes widened. “Bor, is there a half-naked chick sitting there with her hands on me?”

“Yeah. Don’t worry. You are naked, too.”

Borik stood behind her and observed.

The medics crashed into the clearing a moment later and got Del on a gurney.

“Take it easy with him. He is settling in.”

They gave her a series of nervous glances but carried Dolin off through the woods.

Sophy got to her feet and shook the bloody fabric away from her legs.

“So, not that I am complaining, miss, but who are you?”

Borik was standing there, his arms crossed, with a smile on his face and only the healing wounds on his body.

"Oh, Sophia DeMonstre. The Cursed One. Your father called me, but he was setting me up. I had to distract him, but he should be fine. Just called him an ambulance before I came in here."

Her tongue ran away with her as she spoke to him. It always did when confronted with attractive, naked guys built of muscle and magic.

He extended his hand. "Thank you for coming. May I know what you did?"

"Sure. Just let me get my things." She clambered up the rock and got her blades. She was happy she didn't have to stab Dolin to get him to die. It was always easier when she didn't have to kill directly.

She slung the leather strips over her shoulders and smiled at him. "Let's go."

She jumped to the ground, and he led

the way out of his maze and back to the house.

She stopped at her car, opened the trunk, stowed the weapons and pulled on a sports bra and a long tunic. Once they were on, she removed her bloody clothing and put it in a bag for laundering when she got home.

A few wet wipes, set of leggings and sneakers and she was comfortable again.

Borik watched every moment, stark naked and comfortable in his own skin.

She smiled. "Right, so you know that your family carries the minotaur curse."

"Of course."

She leaned against her car. "Well, the curse was never meant for twins, and your mother's family carried a special style of twins. Split souls. You and your brother were literally the same person living in two different bodies. Normally, one twin kills the other in childhood. It is classified as accidental and no one bats an eye. The twin parent is usually able to cover the death, but if not, a visit to the Mage Guild usually clears things up. Bloodlines have a tell; the split soul belongs to the Yorful."

"My brother and I always got along."

"I know, and that is because of your father's curse. Until you were adults, things would have been fine. When you took on the curse—happy birthday by the way—the transformation was split. No control, no humanity or thought when you were in the minotaur form, just animal instinct."

Borik smiled. "So, you knew how to fix that?"

"Your father tried to trap you two, using me as bait. I didn't go for that, and that is why your father needed the ambulance."

"What did you do?"

"Punched him in the groin, hard. In explanation, he had tried to drug me in order to use me as bait. I took exception to that, but I didn't kill him."

Borik blinked. "You punched..."

"Yeah. Not my finest moment, but he is a little bigger than I am. The cheap shot is usually the most effective."

He frowned. "What about Del?"

"Dolin's body holds his recent memories. The cells hadn't begun dying yet. I called a loose, unlinked soul and used it to restart him."

"Loose soul?"

She twisted her lips. "Babies die all the time. After they are born or even before. These souls are unformed by life, and they can be caught and given a second chance before they return whence they came. I called a pure soul and offered it your brother's body. His memories are already there, so the binding is taking hold."

"Will he be himself?"

"As much as you are living with the

curse in your blood."

"It will take some adjustment for me to feel like myself again. I can feel the bull in my blood."

She smiled slightly. "And so it will be for your brother, learning to feel without wondering whether it will be him or you for the change."

"He is going to be a doctor." Borik smiled.

"What were you in school for?"

"Law. I don't think that is a good vein for me now."

She grinned. "You might want to take up accounting. A lot less drama when you lose your temper."

"I will consider it. Will you come inside?"

"No, I think that the moon is rising, and I need to check my phone. Full moons are buggers for curses. Everybody wants to play with magic."

She nodded her farewells, got into her

car and watched his muscled backside stalk into the house. It was a shame to go, but she was too old for him. Cougar had never been in her job description.

Pity.

Chapter Four

Two cursed Ouija boards and one ring later and she dragged herself into her house.

The shower was definitely called for. She was covered in slime from an exploding orb and deeply resenting the ancestor who saddled her with the curse.

Delwin's room was dark, and she went past it, waiting until she got into the bathroom before she stripped to the skin to survey the marks of an active evening as the Cursed One.

Her wounds were healing, but that didn't make them hurt any less.

She had untangled three humans from disaster, and all she had gotten to show for her efforts were screams, slashes and shrieked curse words. Her job sucked.

Her clothes hit the floor with wet splats. She gathered them up and dropped them down the laundry chute.

Her shower had a bar of spray nozzles that hit her from all angles. It was a necessity.

She was scrubbing at her hair when Delwin waltzed in, his pajamas riding low on his hips.

"What is that smell?"

"Necrotic slime." She kept scrubbing from the top down.

"Sophy! What happened to you?"

"Oh, whips of the undead. Not particularly fun."

"The marks on your arms?"

She rinsed her hair off in the hot spray. "Soul catchers. What do you want, Delwin?"

"Can I bring dates over?"

She dumped a squirt of body wash onto a scrubbing puff. "Sure. If they have no ill intent, they can pass through the doorway at your side; send me an email so I set the wards in the morning."

Delwin blinked. "Do you always look like that when you get home?"

"With this much activity, I can usually barely move when I get home. Was there something else?"

He scowled. "Give me that scrub."

She blinked, and he crowded into her shower, kneeling and carefully scrubbing her from shoulder to heels.

"Turn."

She rotated toward him, and he scrubbed carefully around her body and removed all of the traces of muck, dirt and anything else.

"This looks dangerous, Sophy."

"I managed to wrangle you, Delwin. Of course, it is dangerous. You were not even close to the deadliest thing that I went after, venomous or not."

He got up with his pajama pants sodden. "There, all clean. There were some spots that you would never have reached in that shape."

She wrinkled her nose. "Thank you, but this won't give you a break on your rent."

He laughed. "I have figured out a job to apply for."

She raised her brows, naked and nearly chest to chest with him. "Do tell?"

"I think you need a housekeeper. I can stay with you, do laundry, learn to cook, and in exchange, all I want is free rent for a few months."

She poked him in the chest and narrowed her eyes. "I will think about it."

"If I get the stains out of all your clothing, will you do it?"

She wrinkled her nose. "Yes. Now, hand me a towel and stop coming into my bathroom!"

He laughed, peeled off his pajamas, grabbed one towel for her and one for him. With the fluffy white fabric around his hips, he gathered his pants and left.

She called out, "Delwin!"

He turned around warily. "What?"

"Thanks for scrubbing my back."

He winked. "Any time, as long as I don't have company. Skin like yours doesn't deserve that kind of punishment."

"Don't worry. I will be healed in the morning."

He called out over his shoulder. "I was talking about your body wash."

He closed the door behind him, and she was left fighting exhausted laughter.

It seemed that once you let a merman into your home, you were stuck with him.

She wished that he had come with an instruction book.

Yawning her way through reports the next morning, she looked at the approaching cup of coffee with relief. "Thanks, Mom."

"Go home, Soph. We will take care of it." Her mom handed it over with a grin.

"I have the first quarter up to date, filed my reports from yesterday and am due for a visit to the estate shops." She slurped at the coffee without hesitation. It burned slightly, but she gulped it down.

"So, is that merman still living with you?" Her mom's eyes were gleaming.

Sophy wrinkled her nose. "Yes. He is now my official housekeeper. He's going to run my errands and cook for me. Well, he will cook once he learns how. Fortunately, some of his new boyfriends seem to have useful talents in the kitchen."

"Does he do laundry?"

"I find out tonight. The deal is set if

he can get the slime and ectoplasm out of my outfit from yesterday. If he manages it, he can stay."

"Good. You need a roommate. He is as good as any, and he already knows about what you do, so it will be an easier transition for both of you."

"Mom, he is threatening to replace all of my bath products."

Lillian cackled. "Good. You make a ton of money. You should spend part of it on yourself."

"I do. I spend a ton on clothing."

"Stuff that gets destroyed doesn't count. If you can't nap, try and get a training session in."

"Yes, Mom." She handed the empty cup back and cleared up her desk, standing slowly with only a little wincing.

"What did you do last night?"

"There was a spectral lash involved. It takes me longer to heal from those."

"Oh, baby. You have to be more careful."

"I was careful; it hit me and not the humans behind me." She stretched and smiled again. "I will be fine."

She paused. "Mom, did you ever hear of a mage named Magnus who was arrested by the guild?"

"No... not unless you mean Lord Magnus the soul hunter. He was a character and ended up in amber."

"What's the story there?"

Her mother scowled. "I am not sure. I could look into it if you want me to."

"No. I don't think that will be necessary. I will get some more details before I go digging. It isn't a time-sensitive project."

She walked around her desk, gave her mom a kiss and headed for the door, her purse over her shoulder.

Despite her bravado, Sophy *hurt,* and her mom could see it. Soph could only imagine how it had been for her mother to be with her father during his missions. The DeMonstres were genetically programmed to be bait. Being the spouse of one would mean that the person you loved would constantly be in danger.

Sophy didn't date much and that guilt was the reason. You couldn't kiss someone goodbye and have them waiting for you to come home bloody and torn up. It wasn't fair.

She got into the car and buckled up, wiping at the tear that had crept out of her right eye. Damn, she was in rough shape if she was crying.

"Sophia, is something wrong?"

"Nope. Where are you watching me from?" Her phone was in her purse.

"Your GPS."

She pinched the bridge of her nose to stop the tears. "I am fine. I have my rounds today. You can go to neutral or whatever you do when I am not there."

"I am always waiting for you."

"That's creepy." She headed for the estate shop.

"That is my existence. Though, I am happy that they assigned me to your service."

She grimaced. "I thought you were a ghost."

"I am a consciousness. Ghosts can't travel from technology to technology."

Sophy grinned. She had been told. "Why did they send you to me anyway?"

"Because they were tired of doing the referencing for you. Keeping an archivist on duty for hours was far from a desira ble event. They decided that I could be trusted to act as your liaison. I have enjoyed it. You are the first person I have spoken to in centuries."

"Well, we have a half-hour drive. What can you tell me about yourself?"

"I am no longer in physical form." Magnus chuckled.

"Yeah, I know that. How did you come to be hanging out in my GPS?"

Magnus sighed. "I am confined in amber with my magic and soul suspended for my crimes. When I was free, I had a skill with the histories, so when they were looking for someone to act in this capacity, my name arose. The seers were shocked, but the guild agreed to let me out... so to speak."

"What did you do?"

He chuckled. It was a nice sound. "I committed the cardinal sin of deceiving the Mage Guild. I was not what they thought I was, and when I was discovered, the result was my incarceration."

"What did you hide?"

"That is a conversation for another day. Now, why were you crying?"

She thought back to what had started the conversation. "Oh, I was just thinking about how hard it is to be the spouse of the Cursed One. My mom has the patience of a saint."

"Didn't she go on assignments with your father?"

"She did, but once I was there, she didn't."

"Your ancestresses always went to the curses with their children strapped to them. Their husbands kept track of the children while they worked, but the moment they were done, they were back with their families."

"Huh. That was a class that was missing while my father trained me."

Magnus paused. "Ah, I have just located his mother's file. She died young for a Cursed One. She had a sister, though."

"Yes. She taught me blade work. My father was not encouraging me to follow the dictates of the curse."

Magnus snorted. "Foolish. You were doomed to it the moment you were born."

"Gee. Thanks." She snorted.

"It is the truth. I am surprised that there is a surviving DeMonstre who has not taken on the duty of the Cursed One."

"Great Aunt Sapphire is in a wheelchair. She was injured when I was seventeen. She tried to help with the duties, but she was a librarian by nature. A curse blew up in her face, and she has spent the remainder of her life chasing me and trying to get me to continue the family line."

"I have been updating myself on current social behaviours. Don't you like men?"

"I don't want to be wanted for my bloodline, and I don't want to use someone as a breeding stud just because it is time."

"A very grown-up answer."

She laughed. "I have entered my fourth decade. I am a grown up, despite appearances."

She pulled into the parking lot outside the estate shop. "Well, as entertaining as this has been, I have to go work. Please transfer yourself to my phone."

"Yes, Sophia."

She could hear the urge to continue in his voice and the frustration that she cut the conversation off.

She unbuckled, grabbed her purse and left her car. It was time to look through the extensive inventory of Ambermarle Estate Brokers.

Part of her was still girly enough to enjoy shopping.

Chapter Five

 ood day to you, Justin." Sophy smiled at the younger member of the Ambermarle family.

"Madam DeMonstre! I wasn't expecting you." He cleared his throat and looked nervous.

She looked at his body language and flexed her hands. "What came in and where are you hiding it?"

"Um, nothing... Dad, look who is here."

She turned to Ambermarle senior. "Ah, Guy. So happy to see you."

"Madam DeMonstre... what brings you here today?" Guy Ambermarle looked at her and ran a nervous hand over his thinning hair.

Sophy wondered if the hairstyle was genetic. Junior and senior were wearing the same slicked-back style.

"Oh, you know. Just looking for a comb for my hair, and it is time for your inventory check. You know the drill." She quirked her lips.

"Of course. Of course. This way to the quarantined arrivals." He waved her into the depths of the shop stacked with ancient woods, books, statues and instruments.

The estate brokers had been created to keep entire collections of magical artifacts from reaching untrained humans and unsuitable species. Cursed items were common. Most families just locked them up and forgot about them until great uncle or aunt whatever passed away.

She flicked her vision into seeking the chaotic patterns of cursed objects, and she spotted three near the wrapping table, which meant that they would be going out to a client.

"Gee, Guy. You must have been a little out of practice. Those objects haven't made it through quarantine."

He blinked, and the stench of sweat began to creep through his clothing. "Really? They have been here for months."

"I was here four weeks ago, and those items were not here in the shop. What are you up to, Guy?"

"Nothing. I swear. The client was very specific in getting those items, untampered with."

She wandered over to the candlesticks and lifted two of them, whispering to them and dispersing their magic. The saltcellar was particularly nasty. She discharged the magic with a few small words, and the puff of black hate shot upward.

When she was done, she wiped off her fingers and took a photo of the collection. "Note for the file. Items have been cleared of noxious influence."

The words printed across her screen, and she turned back to the shopkeeper with a bright smile. "Now, on to quarantine."

He was blanched and swallowing, but he led her to the rear of the storage area where the chained area told her she was about to go through a busy day.

"Whose estate was it?"

"Leonard Doringer. We got it two weeks ago and have been waiting for your arrival. There is a high demand for many of his works and objects."

She mentally whistled. "Unlock it and give me the key. I will let you know when I am done."

He drew a key with a scarlet ribbon from his pocket and unlocked the cage. She took the key from him when the door of the cage opened, and she stepped inside.

Sound from the shop ceased, as did the world outside the quarantine area. Getting a space warded with dampening magic was expensive, and Sophy really wasn't surprised that the Ambermarles were turning to grey-market cursed goods.

The spell books and enchanted objects were fine. She was specifically looking for items that could embed themselves in a human soul and take hold.

The flare of acid green got her attention. She took out her phone and snapped a photo before she worked on deciphering the curse on the flute.

The flute seemed to be a standard luck-draining curse, but the case was another matter.

"This is new." She took photos of the case and worked on analyzing the spell that stuck to it.

"Magnus, run a check on curse-generating objects."

"Working."

She set the flute back into the case and closed it, keeping the box near her. It was coming with her all cursed up.

The rest of the collection was shockingly benign. Some fatal serving ware was all that needed her attention.

She knew that this was only part of the collection, and she kept the flute case under her arm when she left and locked up the quarantine.

Guy was waiting nervously by the shipping area.

"Okay, Guy. Show me the books. There were at least seven famous objects in the collection that were suspiciously missing."

"I don't know which those could be?"

"Show me the books, Guy, or the guild will be here in an hour."

He pulled the shipping logs down and

laid them out on the table. She flipped through to the last page and found the items in question. Four different collectors, none of whom was human. "Of course."

She took photos of the manifest, checked her image and gave Guy a dark look. "Congratulations. You just bought yourself a weekly check."

His shoulders slumped. "I thought you were coming tomorrow."

She sighed. "I was going to, but I still would have known the objects were missing. I have been to Leonard Doringer's home with my great aunt. I know what he had and what was entailed to other family. This flute is the only object that I need to take away with me, so you are getting off with a warning regarding the stuff you were shipping. Now, I am off to demand those missing items from your clients, so you had better prepare for that."

He shuddered nervously. "I will pre-pare for the fallout."

"Good. I will deal with what is going on with the Doringer collection." She held up the box. "I would like to make sure that I sign this out. If I can return it to you, I will."

He scowled. "What is that? I don't remember seeing it."

"It is a flute."

"It wasn't on the manifest."

She snorted. "It isn't mage magic. It was probably hiding."

Gratifyingly, he didn't ask her how she had seen it. He just wrote a receipt for the flute, and he kept a copy while giving her one.

"What estates do you have coming in?"

"The Meldon collection, as well as the furniture from Imrick the Bold."

"Good. I will be here next week. Keep it in quarantine until I clear it."

She reached into her purse and wrote a clearance for all items in quarantine with the exception of the items previously mentioned. It was important to keep records. When she was done, she signed it, folded her copy and handed the other copy to him.

"There you go. I am going to do a quick run through, just in case."

"Of course, Madam DeMonstre. Thank you for the clearance."

She inclined her head. "Thank you for your cooperation."

Sophy went through the inventory with her senses open wide. Two small bookshelves that would cause confusion were easily dealt with, and the rest were clear.

When she left, she felt the relief in the father and son. She didn't blame them. This was a stopgap measure to slow the cursed objects entering the city. Nothing would stop them, but you could slow them down. Collectors would still collect, and those with evil intent would still find some way to curse their targets. More cursed objects were born every day.

She put the box in her passenger seat and asked Magnus, "Well? Anything in response to my request?"

"Four objects and each is tainted with demon magic."

"Fan-fucking-tastic." She looked at her phone. "Can you dial the Ganger house for me?"

"Done."

She held the phone to her ear and smiled when she heard a familiar voice. "Hello, Lenora, this is Sophy. Can I bring something by and get Emile to take a look at it?"

"Of course, dear. Come over."

"Thank you, Lenora. See you in ten minutes."

She put the car in gear, backed out

and then shifted to drive to the Ganger house. Benny's wedding was just a few days in the past, and Benny herself was now firmly in the XIA.

The time spent around the Ganger family kitchen was a fond memory for Sophy. Her parents and the Gangers were friends of long standing, and that friendship had extended to their daughters.

Benny had taught Sophy so much about identifying power signatures when her father was refusing to help with the training. When her aunt was injured, he changed his mind, and fortunately, her training had occurred without him agreeing to it. Everyone around her had helped her become capable and ready.

The Gangers were like her aunt and uncle. The fact that their home was the largest extranatural research library on the coast made visiting them just a little bit more fun than normal.

"You are familiar with the Gangers?" Magnus sounded surprised.

"Sure. I was at their daughter's wedding a short time ago."

Magnus asked politely, "Will you take me in with you?"

She blinked. "Um, sure. Why?"

"I would like to speak to the current head of the family."

Sophy quirked her lips. "Technically that is Benny, but she is out of town."

"If I may, I would like to speak to the current eldest family member in residence."

"Oh, sure. That is Harcourt Emile. I am not sure which he prefers to go by right now."

"Please allow me to talk with him."

"Well, his wife is also a Ph.D. You might be better off talking to both."

Magnus paused. "Thank you. I will."

Sophy didn't ask why. She didn't need to know.

The drive was completed in silence, and when she left the car, she had her phone in her purse and the box in her arms.

The doorbell rang with an even chime, and Lenora opened the door with a smile. "Sophy, I am so glad you came by. We hardly had a chance to talk at the wedding."

Sophy hugged Lenora and was embraced in return. The box only got in the way a little bit.

"So, what do you have with you?"

Sophia sighed and looked down. "Have you ever heard of demon magic embedding in an object to create curse after curse? This is a curse manufacturer, and I have never seen one before."

Lenora leaned back. "Bring it inside. This is going to take some research. Would you like some cookies?"

Sophy grinned. "Always."

She stepped inside, and the feel of the

house wrapped around her. It welcomed her in a way that only the Ganger home did.

"Harcourt is in the library. I will be in in a minute." Lenora smiled.

Sophy headed for the library and opened the heavy oak doors carved with enough containment glyphs to hide an army.

"Good afternoon, Sophy. You are looking as delightfully young as always." Harcourt glanced up from the tome in front of him, and he grinned at her.

It was weird to see him out of his demon form. His human seeming was handsome, eternally youthful and gave off an attractive aura that was designed to draw men and women in. His incubus form was a little jarring but far more honest in Sophia's opinion.

"You are looking a little pale, Mr. Ganger. It will take some getting used to."

"We have had this discussion. Call me Harcourt." He smiled, and his green and horned form took over. "Thanks for preferring this. The human form is still a little on the difficult side to master."

She knew he was exaggerating and wearing the demon form for her comfort, but she appreciated it.

"Well, funny you should be in demon form. I have come across a curse-manufacturing article, and it is stamped with demon magic from top to bottom."

He extended his hand. "May I?"

"Of course." She held out the box, and he took it in his elegantly scaled hand.

Lenora came in and grinned. "Thank goodness. He was having a problem holding it today. Benny is on an assignment involving radio silence, and he is worried."

Sophia smiled. "I am no seer, but I think Benny will be fine."

Lenora put down a tray of cookies,

and a pitcher of milk was next to it.

"What does it look like, dear?" Lenora walked up to it, her hand extended to caress the wood.

Harcourt jerked it away from her. "Don't touch it, darling. It has a powerful attraction charm on it. This is impressive work. Sophia. Have you tried to break it down?"

"No. I wanted to know what it was first. I tend not to disenchant things unless I am sure of the initial charms."

He smiled. "Smart. This is the work of layers of spells. A millefiori of enticement and evil."

He muttered, "I need to check something."

He held up a hand and whistled sharply. A book whizzed through the air and smacked into his palm. He repeated the gesture again and again until there was a stack next to him. With a low hum, he started to filter through books written in demon languages that Sophia couldn't even see properly. The words blurred and shifted as she observed.

Lenora smiled. "He will be busy for hours. You have something else you wished to discuss?"

"Well, not me precisely."

Lenora raised her elegant brows. "Really? Who precisely?"

Sophia fished her phone out of her purse and put it on the table. "The Mage Guild gave me a liaison in the form of a consciousness named Magnus. When he learned I was coming here, he wanted to speak with you."

Lenora took the phone with a grin. "Hello, Magnus. I am Lenora Ganger. Pleased to meet your acquaintance."

"I am delighted to be in your company, Lady Ganger. I have a query to put to you, and I would like you to answer me out of Sophia's hearing. Would you remove me, please?"

Sophia was curious, but she told Lenora, "He has to be within ten feet of me. I will take the cookies behind the study door."

"No, that is too far. I will just put up a shield of silence."

Sophia nodded and smiled. "Or I can just put in my headphones and some music."

Lenora winked. "That works too."

Sophia sat with her headphones in, music playing, eating cookies and drinking milk while the Gangers worked on her project and her partner.

Lenora did make damn fine cookies.

Chapter Six

Harcourt got her attention with a smile on his demonically handsome face.

Sophia pulled out her earphones. "Did you find something?"

"I found the architect." There was a definite smug air to him.

Sophy could hear the other two conversing a few yards away, but she focused on the book that he was pointing to. A scholar demon was featured in the image, but the lettering wavered and danced.

"I can't read it."

He smiled. "May I touch you?"

"Certainly, just keep it above the

98

equator." She winked, and he touched her hand, holding it in his as he lifted it and pressed it to the page.

She shivered as the words in demon script wavered and became clear.

Arion, the architect of chaos, prince of the demon zone, son of Orbithon the wild king of the outlands.

Arion is an elder prince who gains his power by pulling energy from humans via the curses he has crafted and spread across the earth.

A master of creating debilitating spells and curses, Arion has not been seen since the sixteen hundreds. His touch continues to be felt on the earth in the humans that fall to his curses and surrender to chaos in exchange for power.

Any of his objects should be considered extremely dangerous and not be handled without protection. The en-

chantments he used are insidious and can even affect a demon of any bloodline.

She continued to read minor details about his use of humans for sex in exchange for cutting them free of his charm. He rarely obliged, keeping them in his thrall for years or until they expired.

"That is one creepy son of a bitch."

"I would have to agree. This is his father." He lifted her hand from the page and pulled another book onto the first.

When her hand hit the page, the image of the deep blue demon with a huge rack of stag horns with yellow eyes was glaring at her from a page made of some kind of skin.

"Orbithon is an ancient demon king who wandered into the wilds of the demon zone, appearing periodically to procreate and consume the magic of humans. His lust for power and flesh knew no bounds, and he was shunned by his own kind."

Harcourt continued, "He walked with the undead and consumed the souls of all that crossed his path. When he withdrew from view four hundred years ago, he swore to return when his sons had accumulated enough power to drive his control over humanity and subdue the extranatural community."

"Where did he go?" She glanced at the box on the table.

"The wilds of the demon zone. It is where most of my kind are banished. If he retreated willingly, he had a plan, and a demon with a plan is the most terrifying of its kind."

He released her hand, and the demon disappeared from the page.

"Well, that's terrifying. It has been a few years since I tangled with demon energy."

"Lenora can walk you through it. Your curse will take over once you are given the wherefores of how to tear demon magic apart."

She blinked. "Seriously?"

"Of course. She has known for years how to take demon energy apart. However, as she is now powered by it, I would beg you to be very careful where you aim your spell work."

She nodded. "Of course. I will be careful. I won't even do the work in the house. I just need to see the theory."

He smiled and she swayed back. Wow, the incubus attraction was quite strong.

Harcourt frowned and shifted back to human. "Apologies. Are you finally mature?"

She blinked. "Yeah. I have been for nearly twenty years."

He chuckled and shook his head. "Not that. I mean are you finally of breeding inclination."

Sophia blushed but answered him frankly. "I have been thinking about it lately."

He sighed. "You grew up so quickly. It seems that just yesterday you were with Benny and playing chess in the corner."

She smiled. "I was older than Benny, and we weren't playing chess; she was showing me defensive potions and describing how they were made and where to purchase them."

"I know, but I told your father you were playing chess."

She laughed. "Right. Do you think they are finished?"

He glanced over at Lenora. "You mean my wife and your phone? They look like they are winding up, though she has a stack of books that would choke a horse."

Sophy smiled. "Right. Well, I am going to go break it up. I need her expertise."

"She will be happy to help, but take some cookies, because I am going to eat the rest." He winked.

She grabbed three more cookies and her glass of milk before she headed over to Lenora's desk. "Excuse me, may I cut in?"

Magnus chuckled. "Yes, though it seems odd to be on the other side of that query."

"Welcome to the modern age. Speaking of, I need to charge the phone or your little jaunt will come to an end."

She grabbed the power bank from her purse and aligned the plug, setting the connection in place.

Magnus rumbled. "That feels oddly intimate."

Sophy blushed. "Don't be like that or I won't charge you in public anymore."

She triggered the power bank, and the lights told her that it was working.

She looked at Lenora, who had watched the whole conversation with a smile. "I need to ask you about working with demon magic."

"You don't work with it; you avoid it."

Sophy sighed. "I know, but I need to peel off the layers of magic and destroy the enchantment on that box. I will do it away from here, but I need to know how to crack that first layer."

"I can help with that. Do you know what kind of demon cast the spell?"

"I do."

"Excellent." She raised her hand, and a book four inches thick thudded into her palm. "The answer is in here. Either you can study the tome here, or you can take it home. The choice is yours."

Sophy drummed her fingers on the journal, getting a feel for the book. "If it is safe for me to remove from the library, I will take it."

"It is fine. Only a mage can read it,

and only one with elf blood can make sense of it. You will be fine."

"That is strangely specific."

"It was written by your ancestress, Sapphire deMonstre. You are definitely the audience that she had in mind."

Sophy looked at the book under her hands and opened the first page. The family crest and ancient spelling was central and glowing in illuminated script. She smiled at the slight change in the family name that meant so much to the modern world. It messed up online searches for one thing. She smirked and kept stroking the page.

"How did you get this?"

"Your father brought it here for safe-keeping when you were two. If he died in the line of duty, he wanted someone to protect that bit of family history and give it to you when you came looking for some of the information that the modern age may have lost. Whatever you need to know, the book can tell you."

Sophia ran her hands over the pages as she turned them, reading the words written in a feminine hand. She teared up a little as she read the forward of the first woman to be born a Cursed One.

The pages in this volume contain the knowledge that I have gleaned through years of study. As I approach my two hundredth year, I hope to have time to contain all that I have learned and practiced for generations to come.

I am my mother's daughter, but the skills with magic that have been gifted to me far outstrip her power. It is my observation that the following generations get stronger as we go. My granddaughter is stronger than her mother and myself, and so, I feel that in a few hundred years, the deMonstre line will be one of the most powerful in the world of mages.

The thought of my daughters reaching into the future is my one remaining joy.

The signature was proud. *Sapphire deMonstre Kairo.*

Sophy touched the signature and felt a tingle of power going up her arm from the letters on the page.

"Wow. This is... thank you, Lenora."

"It is my pleasure to give you what is yours. Can you scan the library for any cursed objects?"

"Aside from the usuals?" Sophy smiled.

Lenora blinked. "We have usuals?"

"Sure. Three books on the top shelf. The dagger on the stand in the corner. That wooden bookstand, and..."she pursed her lips as she turned around. "That bell on the third shelf next to the door."

Harcourt lifted his head from the

book on demons. "Really?"

"Yeah. Did you want me to take care of them?"

"Identify the curses first, please."

She walked up to the bell and analyzed it. "When you ring it, the more you need someone to come to you, the quieter the bell rings and the more of a repulsion field it creates. It is more a nuisance than anything else."

The spell work was quiet, and a few whispers shattered the curse into a thousand glittering pieces of dust that exploded in a short purple flame.

"The bookstand is confusion. Simple one. Very annoying to scholars but not fatal."

A small prick of her finger and a drop of blood broke the curse.

Blood was the key to the dagger as well. She offered it to the curse that would poison those who touched it with a slow fever and wasting sickness. Three slow drops of blood on the hilt cracked the curse, and she used magic to peel it off and discard it in an orb that let the magic burn out inside it.

"Okay, the three are cursed as a set. I will bring them down, but you will have to let me know if they have more value while dangerous or as disenchanted."

She walked over to the books and pulled them down. The magic hissed, and the books twisted in her hands.

"Spell of confusion, obfuscation and dangerous arrogance. Interesting combination. The contents are not affected. The binding is where it all lies. So, with your permission?" She didn't wait for more than a nod.

She extended her hands and sent a light sheet of magic toward the books; it wrapped around the books and bled off the power. When the magic was in the layer she had provided, she pulled the layer off and bundled it again. Collecting the spell before she blew it up was a habit, but when the explosion hit, it knocked her on her ass.

She watched it turn to vapour right before she passed out.

Sophia woke up in a chair with Lenora pressing a cold cloth to her forehead. "You have been working too hard."

She struggled to sit up straighter, and Dr. Ganger held her back with surprisingly easy strength.

"What happened?"

"Your wards weren't thick enough, and you compressed the curse too tightly. You made a bomb."

Sophy looked around. "Did it cause damage?"

"Only to you. I have called your parents. They are on their way over."

She tried to put her hand over her eyes, and Lenora held her hands down.

"Don't touch your face, Sophy. You

are crusted with the shattered wards."

Sophy relaxed. "Shit."

"That would be easier to get off. I have never seen solid magic like this before. That is saying something."

The world looked brighter through the crystalline haze that covered her. She lifted her hands and cursed. "Well this bites."

"Stay still. If you dissolve your wards now, you will be coated in the curse, and I don't want that to happen until your father is here to deal with it."

Harcourt was nearby in earnest conversation with Magnus, explaining the situation. It looked strange to see someone talking so seriously to a phone, but she had seen weirder things.

Magnus said, "Show her to me."

Bemused, Harcourt lifted the phone with the charging cable attached and aimed the camera at Sophy.

"That is impressive, Sophy. I have only seen one backfire like it in all my years."

Harcourt carefully set the phone down. "What happened then?"

"Oh, the mage died. You need to get a layer of magic between yourself and the shattered effect as soon as possible."

Lenora nodded. "Right. Let's get you to the workout room."

She moved behind Sophy and helped her up from the chair. "Let me do the work, Sophy. I need you to move slowly from here on out. I can't touch any part of you that has the magic on it."

Sophy nodded and began to move. Each step felt like wading through ice water. Her skin was getting colder with every step. She counted. Twenty steps out of the library. Seventeen steps down the hall and ten more into the room where the experiments were carried out. Nothing was on the walls, and the tile was treated to repel magic. She was in the equivalent of a lead-lined chamber.

With a lot of effort, she boosted herself onto the workbench and focused on analyzing the spell that was on her skin. Her magic was bonded to the residue of the curse, making it hard to focus and giving her the sensation that her own body was repellant.

There was only one thing to do; she had to unravel her own magic.

She picked apart each layer of magic, from the inside out, pressing outward when the curse tried to touch her skin. A swift destruction of the energy and she slumped forward.

"Good job, micro mite." Her father's voice was near her.

"Dad, when did you get here?" Her head was spinning.

"An hour ago, but you were doing fine."

She looked at him through exhausted eyes and smiled. "I think I deserve a cookie."

She slammed her head onto his shoulder on the way down.

Chapter Seven

Delwin was the first face that she saw. He was leaning over her and sponging her forehead.

Sophy blinked. "What are you doing here?"

"Well, I live here. So do you. Your parents brought you in, and your phone gave me instructions on how to take care of you. He is a bossy fella."

Magnus's voice was next to her. "Yes, I am. Such as I am. She needs rest and recuperation."

"She needs folks to stop talking about her like she isn't awake." Sophy tried to sit up and groaned, falling backward.

"As I said. You used a lot of energy,

and your body is recovering. You need a week of nothing but rest." Magnus sounded smug.

"That isn't going to happen. I have duties to execute."

"Your father is resuming the mantle for a week. He is excited." Magnus chuckled. "He and I got along very well."

She ignored that. "He can't. He isn't the Cursed One."

"He was, and that was enough for Lenora to *borrow* the curse for a week. You are free for the next seven days until you are back to full strength."

"Why are you suddenly in charge? You don't even have a body."

Delwin was watching the whole exchange with a grin.

"Because I have seen what you were engaged in before. A blown spell like that should have killed you, but your energy held it and froze around it. You have excellent reflexes but very little preservation instinct."

She grumbled. "I haven't needed it. The curse protects me."

"Not if you are going up against demon magic. You are going to need special expertise. I am willing to provide it, for a price."

She looked at her phone and made a face.

"I saw that."

"I could just shut you off."

"I would simply take over another appliance with a camera. Listen to my offer and tell me what you think."

She sat up slowly, and Delwin left her with a wink and a whispered, "You seem to be in good... hands?"

She made another face and looked down at the phone. "What do you want?"

"I want you to petition the Mage Guild for my release. Just one appearance at the Guild Hall and I will tell you what you need to know about dealing with those demon curses."

Sophy sighed. "I thought I was supposed to be resting."

"Ha. Funny. You and I both know you will be on your feet in minutes. Your physical body is fine; it is your magical energies that need to recover."

She groaned and flipped the covers over the phone. She was naked, and he didn't need to see that. Her entire body ached. She moved with glacial slowness to the shower and let the hot water take out the aches and pains that she was feeling. Her body was marked with traces of energy under the skin, marks that looked like rivers of power. "That is new."

When she was wrapped in a towel with her hair mostly dry and draped over her shoulder, she uncovered the phone.

"I already saw you naked. Delwin

helped your mother undress you. It was a delightful show.”

“Perv.”

“I admire the female form and yours more than any other.”

She glared at him. “Stop sucking up. I am feeling stronger. We can go to the Guild Hall today.”

“You might want to wait on that. It is the middle of the night. You have been out for hours.”

She looked to the window and saw the dark of night outside. “Well, fuck.”

She lifted her blankets, crawled back under the sheets and pulled the towel away when she was done settling. Time for another nap. If she was honest, she needed it.

“You know you always curse when you are thwarted.”

She pulled her duvet up next to her ear. “I know.”

Delwin crept into the bedroom when he felt Sophia had fallen asleep. He removed the charger from her phone and removed the item from her bedroom.

Outside in the hall, he made sure he was a sufficient distance before he asked the phone. "Who the hell are you?"

The rich voice was challenging. "Who are you? I was under the impression that Sophia was not in a relationship."

"I am her housekeeper and roommate. My name is Delwin. My question stands."

"Magnus. I am her liaison to the Mage Guild. I occupy her electronics, but normally, she turns her phone off when she goes home."

"Where's your body?"

"It is a long story."

"What can you tell me about what she

likes?" Delwin finally came out with it. "She is a fussy eater, and I don't know what her favourites are."

"You are joking."

He cupped the phone between his palms and whispered, "No. I like it here, and I don't want to move. I want to keep her happy."

The phone sighed. "Cookies, tacos, soda, spicy and sweet. Those are her favourites. Now, please, put me back. I would like to be there when she wakes."

"So, you have a body."

"Yes. It is just not accessible to me right now. Sophia is going to assist me with that."

Delwin was suddenly suspicious. "Does she know she is helping you?"

A flash of light struck him.

Delwin walked away from Sophia's room wondering what he had been doing there. He could have sworn that he was going to ask the phone something, but now, he couldn't remember what that was. Ah, well, it probably wasn't important.

Sophia kept her bedding over the phone while she got dressed.

She smoothed a long, brilliant-blue, split-side tunic down over her black leggings and slipped her feet into some wedge heels. Her hair was in a smooth ponytail that hung down her back. Modest earrings and a matching necklace were in place before she unwrapped the phone.

"I can't do anything, even if I see you naked."

She snorted. "A girl has secrets. I have more than most."

She held the phone and got her purse.

The moment she stepped into the hallway, the scent of oatmeal and cinnamon assailed her nostrils.

She followed the scent into the kitchen where Delwin was setting out a plate of oatmeal cookies next to a stack of napkins.

"I figured you might want to get going right away, so I made these so you can take them on the road. They are fortified with seeds and nuts as well as a hefty dose of chocolate chips and raisins."

He paused and blinked. "Oh and oats."

She smiled. "Thank you. That is really thoughtful. How did you know I like all of my food in cookie form?"

He chuckled. "I have no idea. It just came to me in the night."

Sophy heard a snort from her purse.

She grabbed a stack of cookies and folded them in a napkin. "These look great."

"Let me know if you want me to change anything." He smiled brightly, and his green-tinged skin glowed with a blush.

Sophy nodded and headed for the door.

She heard him call out. "Wait!"

To her shock, he had a thermal mug in his hand, and the smell was coffee.

"Wow. Thanks. Have a good day, Delwin."

He smiled brightly and returned to the house, humming a tune with all three sets of his vocal chords.

Sophy didn't know what to say about that, so she got in her car and started driving.

"Are you having sex with the merman?"

She scowled at the GPS unit. "Of course not. He prefers men."

"Ah. That was not made clear."

"Why would it be any of your business? Delwin is perfectly nice as long as you don't have a tub he wants to flip his tail out in."

"I see."

"Not if you were with me you didn't." She snickered. "He tends to leave traces of scale behind. I am guessing that he wants to soak to shed the old scales."

"Why doesn't he scrub in the sea?"

She wrinkled her nose. "I think he has developed a phobia regarding open water. He only frequents pools now. It is a little sad."

Magnus was quiet. "What is your destination?"

"I am going back to the Gangers' to get the cursed box, and then, I am going to put it in the trunk while I go to the Mage Guild headquarters."

"You are going to speak to them today?"

She chuckled. "I have a day off. Trust me. It does not happen often."

When she got to the Gangers' home, she rang the bell and smiled when Lenora answered the door with her hair and clothing askew.

"Pardon me, Lenora. I just came to retrieve the cursed case and flute. If I can just grab them, I will let you and Harcourt continue your... meeting?" She grinned wide.

Lenora sighed. "Come in. We were in the kitchen, so the library is safe. We put a cloche over the case, just so we wouldn't handle it by accident."

Sophy stepped inside as Lenora stepped back. "I will get it out of your hair."

They walked down the hall to the library. They entered and Lenora continued, "How are you feeling?"

"Better. I hear that you put Dad on duty again."

"I did."

"And I bet he was delighted." She

chuckled and removed the heavy glass dome from the case. She tucked it under her arm and nodded to Lenora. "Thanks for hanging on to this."

"Well, we weren't going to touch it. Demon magic is stickier than hell, so to speak."

"Right. Well, I am off to the Guild Hall, so I will check in and see if any of them have heard of this kind of thing before."

Lenora frowned. "You are not bringing it into the hall."

"Nope. It will be all safe and warded. Do not worry." She smiled. "Thanks for babysitting it and giving my dad the vacation he is desperate for."

"I transferred the curse."

"And he is enjoying himself." She didn't mention that she could feel her father's joy through the spot that the curse occupied.

"Well, dear, have a good day. I have to

get back to Harcourt. He is shackled to the stove."

Sophy felt her eyes widened. "I have nothing to say to that. Have fun, you two."

She didn't flee the Ganger home, but she didn't waste time. She was back in her car and driving to the Guild Hall in under a minute.

"Your trunk is warded?" Magnus was nosy today.

She sighed and put her blinker on. "Of course. With all the gear I haul around, it is essential that it is protected against search and seizure, as well as those who would seek out the power or supplies." She smirked. "I also have a few changes of clothing back there, and that is hard to explain when pulled over. The armament doesn't even make a dent on their awareness when they get a look at the lingerie."

Magnus chuckled. "I can see where

that would be distracting."

"Yeah, and you can't even get an erection."

Sophy enjoyed the blissful silence that her comment caused, right up until she pulled up to the Guild Hall. She was forced to ask, "Who do I have to ask for?"

He answered the words that she was really hoping he wouldn't. "The Archmage."

She dropped her forehead to the steering wheel. "Fuck."

Chapter Eight

She straightened her clothing and grabbed her purse. "Keep quiet, Magnus. I will ask for your release, but that is it."

"It will be enough."

Sophy walked into the building that managed to wedge ancient architecture into a modern office building. It was not a good look. The officers at the door watched as she walked through the scanners and didn't set off the demon scans, so they waved her through.

She had been in the Hall often enough to know where to go, she just didn't want to go there.

A lovely young woman whose gaze

was filled with leashed power manned the reception desk. She was not just decorative. She gave Sophy a speculative look as she approached.

"Good morning, miss."

"Good morning."

"How may I help you?" She folded her hands on the desk. It was not a good sign. Normally, a proper receptionist would have a pen or keyboard under her fingers.

"I need to see the Archmage." The moment she said it, she wanted to take it back and make a beeline for the door.

The receptionist gave her a brittle smile. "He is occupied this morning. May I take a message?"

"Certainly. Please, tell him that Sophia DeMonstre, the Cursed One, is waiting in the lobby, and the more coffee I drink, the worse things will be when he shows up." She smiled tightly as the woman blanched at her words.

"*You* are the Cursed One?" The expression went from contempt to hero worship in an instant.

"I am."

"Oh, I love your work. Just a moment. I will call him."

Sophy waited and actually signed an autograph for the receptionist—Judith—while the woman made the call before Aleneus bolted into the entry hall with his robes swinging and a hectic expression in his eyes.

"Sophia. You are here." He rushed up to her and took her hands, bringing them to his lips one at a time.

"I am. I have something to ask of you. I would rather that it not be done here." She looked around at the curious faces who were watching them intently.

Judith was smiling at Sophia's autograph as they passed her desk with Sophy's hand firmly clutched in Aleneus's.

He had been trying to get her either

into bed or a marriage since she turned eighteen, and as he was only two years older than she was, it was a little disturbing that he hadn't given up in the subsequent decades.

"I am so delighted to see you here, Sophia."

"Oh, it is a delight, all right."

They rode up to his offices in the elevator, and she checked the nearest windows in case she needed to jump. Sure, it was nine stories, but she was betting she could recover from the fall if she could push herself past the wards.

He set her in a curved chair in front of his desk, and he settled in his own chair, steepling his fingers and smiling. "What can I do for you, Cursed One?"

She placed her hands in her lap. "I would like you to release Magnus."

He frowned. "Who?"

"Magnus. The mage in amber whose consciousness is currently haunting my phone and any other appliances with audio capabilities. He is my liaison with the guild, and I would like him released but to remain in the capacity of my advisor." The words came out before she knew what she was going to say.

Aleneus stared at her, his mouth opened and closed, his hands clenched into fists. "Why do you want him?"

Whoa. There was a lot of anger aimed in her direction, but it was about her request and not her personally. He was treating her as if she had been bespelled.

"He has been useful, and if he has served centuries, I believe that he is done with penance. At the very least, he is capable of being integrated into modern society."

Aleneus winced, and she could almost hear the whirring of his mind. "He will be released."

"Wow. That was easy."

"Well, the sentence was that if a

woman that did not have carnal knowledge of him asked for him to be released, he would be. When that regulation was put in, we did not count on his consciousness being pulled for this assignment." He grimaced and pulled a sheet of parchment from his desk.

Everything in the guild was done as traditionally as possible, and that included penmanship.

Aleneus wrote with a flourish; his golden hair fell forward as he finished and sanded the page.

"So, Sophia, what are you doing for dinner this evening?"

Sophy blinked. "I am doing some research at the Gangers."

He grimaced. "Oh. Them."

"Demon influence. I have found a cursed object, and I need to look into it. They are the best source for knowledge and information." She didn't mention that she had already gotten it. He didn't need to know that.

"I would like to take you to dinner soon. You are not getting any younger, and keeping the curse in powerful bloodlines would not be a bad idea."

She blinked. "I had not thought of that. One of my ancestors had their daughter in their fifties, so I have some time."

He scowled. "I want you, Sophia."

"I am aware of that, Aleneus."

"Was that all you wanted?"

Sophia looked at him, truly looked. He had wide shoulders, a very attractive face, thick neck, deep chest and his butt wasn't bad either. He took care of himself, and it showed, but he wasn't for her.

"Yes, that is all that I wanted here." She smiled softly. "Good day, Aleneus." Sophy rose to her feet and headed for the exit.

"I will have to summon you here after

Magnus is free, to make sure that he is behaving."

She paused and turned. "What do you mean?"

Aleneus was standing up, and he crossed his arms over his chest. "Didn't he tell you? By asking for his freedom, you are now responsible for his behaviour, and his behaviour has never been acceptable to the Mage Guild."

She gritted her teeth. "No, he didn't mention that."

"Enjoy your charge. We can put him back in the amber if you say the word."

Sophia nodded and left his offices as quickly as she could. She didn't run but walked swiftly through the halls and tapped her feet in the elevator. The final sprint to freedom concluded in her car when she settled, put on her seatbelt and started up the vehicle.

"Were you going to tell me that I was responsible for you?"

"I hoped but was not sure that they would actually release me. They are doing it?"

She sighed and put her car in gear. "Yeah, weren't you listening?"

"No. My ability to communicate does not extend to the Guild Hall in this form."

She grunted and headed home. It was time to work on the stuff she could actually control. "Did the book come home with me?"

"Yes. It is on the coffee table."

"Good. I have some reading to do while they thaw you out." She mused. "I wonder if I have to pick you up or will they deliver you?"

"I have access to portal magic. I will deliver myself."

"Oh. Yay. Nothing like another surprise to cap the day."

He chuckled, and she fought a smile.

Once home, she startled Delwin, who

had on an apron and was dusting the objects that didn't have repulsion wards. He was taking his duty as a housekeeper seriously.

"I am just going to grab this book and head into the back yard. As you were, Delwin. It is looking great." She smiled.

He grinned. "Thanks, Sophia."

She headed out the back door and saw that he had already cleared her small table and tiny chairs. It was downright cozy now.

The journal welcomed her touch, and she opened it, focusing on information on demon magic, and when the page settled in front of her, she started reading.

Three hours later, she rubbed at her eyes and stretched. It was going to take a few ingredients she didn't have, but she would be able to break through the exterior enchantments. It was a good thing she had a license to purchase the rarer ingredients. That stuff was controlled in many cities, including her own.

Magnus had gone quiet after the first hour. That was probably when she had stopped reading out loud. He had nothing to comment on.

She went inside, got a notepad and pen and returned to the back yard. Time to make a shopping list.

Delwin brought her some lemonade and some small sandwiches.

"It's lunchtime. You need to stay fuelled up."

"Thanks, Delwin. You don't have to do all this." She took the lemonade and sipped at it. "But it is very much appreciated."

He smiled. "I am enjoying it. You very obviously need someone to assist you at home. Now, you just need to find one to help you on the job."

She sighed. "Well, I had an offer today." It slipped out before she could stop it.

Delwin sat across from her. "Who was it? A dashing guild officer?"

She made a face. "Sort of. An old acquaintance."

"Really? Can I ask who?"

Sophy was saved by an arrival on her property. In the far corner of the yard—the only place warded for transport arrival—a large figure took shape before the light faded.

"Oh. I appear to have a visitor."

Delwin was staring at the man, and he sighed. "Oh, if only he was here for me."

She gave him a grin and walked over to the corner where her guest was pinned in the heavy warding. "Hello."

He smiled. "Hello. You are taller than you seemed through the lenses."

The voice made her shiver and coming out of the mouth of a man who looked like he would have an easier time swinging a sword than driving a car, she suddenly realized she had been backed into a corner. "Magnus."

He grinned. His long, dark hair was shaggy and slid forward when he bent his head toward her. His jaw was broad, the blade of his nose was arched and the nostrils flared. It was a serious nose above some very mobile lips. They were currently curved in a smile.

"Sophia DeMonstre. I am here to assist you, as you are my guardian." He inclined his head.

She wrinkled her nose and let him loose from his confinement.

"Pleased to meet you, Magnus. I am still working on that research but was about to go out to get some supplies."

He was wearing contemporary clothing, and he was wearing it well. The jeans and obscenely faithful t-shirt were something she wanted to enjoy looking at, so she decided to avoid them instead.

Sophia returned to her table and made the notes, flipping the pages back and forth until she was sure that she had listed every ingredient that she didn't already have at home.

"May I come with you?" Magnus was into her lemonade and sandwiches.

"Yes. I don't trust you around Delwin. He seems to want to climb you like a stripper pole."

Magnus looked toward the merman, and he smiled. "Well, I must say that he is extremely attractive but, sadly, not my type."

Delwin blushed and scuttled inside, bringing out another lemonade with a smile. "Here you go, sir."

Sophia muttered, "Magnus, his name is Magnus, and according to the Mage Guild, he did something very bad."

Magnus smiled. "According to them. I did something unacceptable by their standards, and my sentence was the amber. Well, until a woman asked for me to be freed who had not had intimate knowledge of my body."

Sophia snorted. "I have never licked my GPS. Not once. Oh, and I gripped my phone but never fondled."

Delwin smiled, "Where is he going to sleep? I vote my room."

Magnus inclined his head. "I can make myself a shelter out here. I am used to living rough, or I was. I am sure I can be again."

Sophy folded her list and put it in her bra. "You will have a problem conjuring anything here. My home is warded against that kind of thing."

"I will make do."

Sophy kept her mind on business, grabbed the book and smiled. "Well, if you have to stay with me, prepare to ride shotgun. We are going shopping."

Magnus followed her into her house, and suddenly, the comfortable space felt a lot smaller.

She locked up the book and grabbed her purse. Magnus extended his hand, and her phone was in his palm. "You almost forgot me."

"This was a perfectly good phone before you inhabited it."

He grinned. "And now it is a great phone."

She grabbed her phone and shoved it into her purse, stalking out the door and leaving him to close up behind her. She had gained an assistant, and she had no idea what to do with him.

Well, she did have a few ideas, but he was sleeping outside, so that wasn't going to happen.

Chapter Nine

Sawberry's Magical Supplies was a huge chain that bragged it had everything in stock.

Magnus whistled slowly. "Are we going in there?"

Sophy chuckled. "No. Follow me."

She locked her car up when they were standing in front of it and turned away from the supply superstore, walking to the blank brick of the building behind it.

She pressed her fingers against the brick and tapped out a code. A doorway appeared. She grabbed Magnus's hand and hauled him with her through the doorway.

The light settled into a very pleasant

room with the air of a library crossed with a tearoom.

The woman behind the counter surprised Sophy. "Minerva? What are you doing here?"

"Oh, Tabeel drank some of her own tea and had to check into the medical centre. She will be fine as soon as she stops burping up fortune-telling bubbles."

Sophy looked at her friend and grinned. "When is she going to learn that she can't try her own concoctions?"

Minerva shrugged and moved to lift a wide box up and over her head.

Magnus moved swiftly and helped her set it in place. Minerva looked up at him. "Well, hello. Friend of Sophia's, I presume?"

"You could say that. She is responsible for me." Magnus smiled down at her. "However, if I had known that there was an enchantress such as yourself behind that wall, I would have beaten it down for the honour of your greeting."

Sophia rolled her eyes, and Minerva grinned.

"You are not from around here, are you?"

"No. I am not. I am a very recent arrival, sworn to the service of the Cursed One."

Sophy snorted. "Nothing like the word *cursed* to make a girl feel special."

Magnus moved from behind the counter and returned to her side. "That is not what I meant."

"You are bound to me. I get it. Now, Minerva, can you help me out?"

Minerva held out her hand. "Give me the list, and I will tell you what is and isn't in stock."

"They should all be fairly standard."

She retrieved the list from her cleavage and handed it over to the most powerful mage of their age. Minerva couldn't just use magic; she could create a new magical ritual and predict the effect. It was one of the greatest talents of the current age.

Minerva was an impressive woman all around. She was the image of an ancient amazon crossed with a giant and blessed with curves. Everything about her was striking, even when she moved to gather the ingredients on the list.

"How long have you known each other?"

Sophy snorted. "She is too young for you, Magnus."

"No. It just seems that you have a camaraderie that is surprising, considering what you are and what she is."

"What? That I am over a decade older than she is? Or is it that I tear magic apart and she creates it?"

He stared at her, at Minerva and back again. "You don't know what her parentage is?"

Sophy shrugged. Fortunately, Minerva was at the far end of the shop. "She's adopted. Nothing more needs to be known. Now, zip it."

He looked like he wanted to fight that comment, but she glared at him.

Magnus quieted as they waited for the list to be gone through. Each item was placed carefully on a separate piece of tissue that would keep them from interacting before it was time.

She bit her lip as she counted and held her breath when there was one item missing.

Minerva tapped the list over and over as she returned to them. "You just need one thing."

Sophy looked at the list and blushed. "Right. I have that at home."

"Thought you might but wasn't sure if it was still good." Minerva folded the list with a smile. "Well, everything else is here."

Minerva packed the items up, one by one, until she had a large bag and a smile. "Nineteen, please."

Sophy reached into her purse and pulled out a small coin canister. She opened one end and poured out the nineteen gold coins. "There you are. Tabeel should be happy. I think I just paid her rent for a month."

"Or, it will pay for her medical treatment. Either way, she will be happy. Have a great day, and we need to go for coffee at the Patchwork Dragon. It's illuminating."

Sophy grinned. "Now that he isn't occupying it, my phone is at your disposal. Call me anytime. I will be only too happy to meet up. This is my first week off in years."

It was about the only thing that could have shocked Minerva. "You have time off? What happened?"

Sophy chuckled and took the bag.

"Call me when you are done here, and I will tell you over coffee."

"Done."

Magnus followed her out of the specialty shop and back to the car. He was still bemused by whatever he had sensed in Minerva.

Sophy didn't blame him; her friend was fascinating. She was the physical embodiment of strength, intelligence, grace and beauty, not to mention power.

She sighed at the fleeting thought that Magnus was the man for her. He obviously didn't return the sentiment.

She put the ingredients in a charmed bag in the trunk, confirmed that the case was still in place and slammed it closed. When she was back behind the wheel, she tempered her disappointment and headed for home.

"What is the missing ingredient? Is it a kitchen spice or something?" Magnus was keeping the conversation light.

"Oh, no. It is just a bit of blood. I forgot that I had some at home."

"May I see the list?" He paused. "Please? I have such knowledge of some of these things."

She fished the list out again and handed it to him.

He went down the list and paused. "Virgin's blood?"

"Yeah."

"And you have some at home?" He raised his brows.

"I do."

"How fresh is it? It must be bright for this to work."

She grimaced. "Oh, it's fresh. That is not the issue."

He chuckled. "Here, I thought that Delwin was more a man of the world."

"He is enjoying his freedom at his own pace."

She continued the drive in relative silence, answering the few questions that he put to her with monosyllabic answers.

Her mind was already on the curse breaking. Some she could do on her own, but others—older curses—required props. The music case was old. The flute looked to be over two hundred and the case might have even changed shape to move with the times.

She pulled into her drive with relief. The sooner she got this over with, the sooner she would be able to recover from her exertion and get back into the curse-cancelling business.

Sophy opened her trunk and reeled a little at the heady scent. "That is some strong frankincense."

Magnus came up beside her. "Allow me."

He pulled the bag out of the trunk, and Sophy cancelled the wards and unlocked the secure storage. The box was right where she had left it and writhing with energy, as if it knew what she had planned.

"Well, it isn't happy. Let's get to the workshop and get this underway."

She closed her trunk and carried the box past the side of the house and into the back yard. The workshop was deceptive. On the surface, it looked like a small shed, but beneath, it ran the length of the block.

It was nice that the houses next to hers were maintained but unoccupied. It would never do to blow up a property that wasn't her own.

"Why are you just following me around?"

"I have never seen someone attempt what you are about to do. It is fascinating."

She wrinkled her nose. "It is my job. I do this, I read books, go for coffee with friends, and then, I do it all over again. In between, I do accounting work for my family."

"What about a lover?" His words were casual.

She laughed all the way to the workshop and down the stairs.

Three hours of pounding, drying and simmering the ingredients and she was ready to let it sit overnight. The herbs had to steep.

She brushed her leather apron and washed her hands. "So, is it any different from your day?"

He held up the coffee grinder. "This is definitely different. It would have saved days of work."

Sophy laughed. "It does. My parents insisted I learn the traditional ways first, but every time I think I can insert the modern world without upsetting the balance of the spell, I do."

He looked around. "Don't you have to add the blood for the steeping?"

She turned scarlet, pulled a dagger from the magnetic strip on the wall and cut her hand.

She muttered as she held her hand over the bowl. "Not pure as the driven snow but where a man has yet to go. Strip the curse against the tide; accept it from the virgin bride."

The nine blood drops fell, and the bowl stirred itself. Sophy wrapped her hand with gauze she kept nearby for just such an occasion, wiped the dagger with alcohol and more gauze and tapped Magnus's mouth to close it.

The dagger went back into place, and she unwrapped her hand to check on the healing.

"You're a virgin?"

She shrugged. "Is it so surprising? My ancestresses and I were all designed to be tempting and youthful. To find a man who looks beyond our beauty is not something that comes easily. I have been looking for decades, and all I have come across is a man who wants me for my power."

He frowned. "I... What I mean to say is—"

She cut him off with a raised hand. "It's fine. I am not your type. Got it. It has been made very clear." She smiled sadly. "It happens all the time."

Her phone buzzed, and she stepped away. "Hello?"

"I am officially off work, and Tabeel has stopped blowing bubbles for the day. I can meet you at the Patchwork Dragon on Merry Street in half an hour." Minerva's voice was tired but chipper.

"Excellent. I will be there. I just need to rinse off some of the herbs, and I will head over."

"See you soon."

Minerva hung up, and Sophy did the same.

She smiled at Magnus. "You are off

shadow duty. Come on back to the house. You can frolic on the internet and enjoy the vast array of extranatural porn."

He cleared his throat. "About what we were talking about before the call. There are reasons for my flirting."

"Excellent. Keep them to yourself. I am very familiar with the signs of a man who has no interest in me. I am fine with it. We both know where we stand."

She tidied up and shooed him up the stairs. She sealed the workshop with a strong locking spell.

Sophy took one look at Delwin dressed for the evening, and she grinned. "You look splendid."

He preened. "Thank you. Magnus, are you interested in coming to a club this evening? There is always room for one more."

Magnus paused. "I thought to go with Sophia."

Sophy shook her head. "Minerva and I want to engage in girl talk. Unless you want to sit at a separate table. You will not be sitting with us."

He wrinkled his nose. "May I decide when you have gotten dressed for the evening?"

She raised her hand and snapped her fingers. The apron disappeared, the scent of herbs vanished and the wrinkles relaxed into a smooth sheet of fabric once again.

"The wonders of modern magic. So, are you coming with me, with Delwin or staying here and relaxing?"

"I have decided to go with you, only because I have spent enough time relaxing, and Delwin looks far too eager to show me off." He inclined his head. "I fear I must request coin of the realm."

Sophy went to the wall, waved her hand and pulled out a stack of bills. She split it in half and handed one to each of them. "Here you go. Do with it what you will. I am heading to the car. If you want to come along, Magnus, you had better be quick."

He was at her side during the drive to the Patchwork Dragon.

Chapter Ten

Minerva grinned at her and casually said, "He is staring again."

Magnus was sitting with a sample of every type of coffee and tea available at the Patchwork Dragon in front of him. The table was covered with little white cups.

The servers were bickering to attend his table as he took sip after sip and made notes on a small piece of paper.

He was looking toward them with a hungry gaze.

"He is staring at you, Min. He and I have already had the talk that firmly lodged him in the friend zone. I am not his type."

Minerva chuckled. "You are nearly every male's type. Even the gay ones want to befriend you. I am pretty sure that you just got some signals crossed."

"I am pretty sure I didn't. Frankly, it was my virginity that put him off. He's repelled by it. Funny, right?" She sighed and sipped at her bowl of cappuccino.

Minerva scowled. "You are kidding."

"Nope. His mouth dropped open."

"I don't know what to say. Perhaps things were dif—no that wouldn't be right. A few hundred years ago, it was a prize."

Sophy shrugged. "I am used to rejection. Once folks realize what I do for a living, I am out on my own. It isn't something that most guys would sign on for."

"Well, I am currently dealing with a similar but opposing situation. I am used to guys running the other way, but an arms dealer is currently after me for sexual purposes."

Sophia blinked. "You are kidding."

"Nope. He is one of the mountain dragons. I was singing a few weeks ago to get a treaty ratified for the goblins, but when it was over, he invited me to dinner."

Sophia winced. "You didn't."

Minerva blushed. "I was hungry. It takes a lot of effort to maintain this figure."

"So, you ate with him, and then, he seduced you?"

"Well, we had sex on the table. I excused myself afterward and made a run for it. The goblins were bound by a geas, and I didn't think he would be able to find me."

Sophy chuckled. "You do stand out, and they track by scent and taste. Body and magic."

Minerva grimaced. "I found that out when I did my research after the encounter. I haven't run into a dragon before. It caught me by surprise."

Sophy thought about it. "Zemuel."

Minerva had a visceral reaction. Her fingers spasmed, she blushed and her pupils dilated. "How did you know?"

"Only so many dragons in North America. He is the only one with mines and property that the goblins would be interested in." Sophy chuckled. "I have worked with him before. He is a good sort, though he does like to collect mages around him. You would have gleamed like a diamond in sunlight to him."

Minerva groaned while Sophy sipped at a bowl.

They laughed, and Sophy gave Min some tips on how to handle a dragon with mating on his mind.

The proprietor was going around the coffee shop, reading cups and telling fortunes. When she got to them, Minerva smiled. "Hiya, Jennifer. Business is booming."

The woman who looked a lot like their friend Benny smiled. "You can't beat the markup on coffee. Would you like a true reading?"

Sophy nodded. "Please."

Jennifer raised her hand, and a server brought Sophy another cappuccino. "Cradle it in your hands and take a sip."

Sophy didn't really want one, but she did as she was told.

When she put the cup down, Jennifer took it and focused on the foam and coffee.

"I see a man in your future, pure and impure. His mark is the spiral horn, but he fights his nature each day. Interesting. Another man with glowing power also calls to you, but he is driven by selfish desires and an urge to collect."

Jennifer blew softly across the surface, raising one hand above the coffee to hold the steam and read it. "You want but can't have. Desire but are rebuffed, and will not chase what you truly seek. You need a partner in all things, but the horned man is fighting you every step of the way."

Jennifer handed her cup back. "You are screwed."

Sophy was startled into laughing. It sounded just like Benny.

Minerva's coffee was in her hands a moment later, and Min's grin faded.

"You are being hunted, and he will catch you. The gods will come at your call, but you will have to choose, sunlight or moonlight, love or family."

Minerva blinked. "Right. Okay."

"Oh, and he will be here in five minutes, so if you don't want to deal with him, I would get going." Jennifer winked.

Minerva was on her feet in a moment. She smiled at Sophy. "Sorry, but I don't want to do this tonight."

Sophy waved her off and gestured for Jennifer to take her place. "Have a seat and take a break."

Jennifer sat with an air of relief. "Thanks. I need this. I swear, I had no idea what I was getting into when I went into partnership and decided to read fortunes as a hook to get butts in the seats."

"You are doing well with your acquired skills. Most folks would have run to another city by now."

Jennifer shrugged. "This is my home. My entire life was skewed by what happened, I am trying to start over, and familiar surroundings are definitely helping. The seer skills are a shock, but I am getting used to them."

"You are doing exceptionally well. I have seen dozens, if not hundreds, of mages and a few seers. Coming into your power is always a struggle."

Jennifer chuckled. "I am just lucky

that Benny had such a strong grip on her magic. That path imprinted on my mind, and I am grateful for it."

"I know she regrets what was done."

"I know it, too. We have had a few long chats, and the court case settled it all. Postpartum depression is a bitch, and it can make mothers do weird things. This was just one of them."

Jennifer looked over to Magnus. "I think he is my next stop. I have noticed him looking at you. Are you two an item?"

Sophy chuckled. "Just work acquaintances. Have at him."

Jennifer pushed herself to her feet and walked over to Magnus. They spoke for a few moments before he picked up a cup, sipped and handed it over.

Sophy nursed her second monster cappuccino while they talked.

She smiled when she saw a familiar face enter the café. The rest of the patrons stopped and stared, but they had reason to. It wasn't every day that the humanish form of a dragon wandered into a coffee shop.

She sipped at her coffee again and watched him approach; his nostrils flared.

He walked right up to Minerva's chair. "How much did I miss her by?"

Sophy simply smiled and sipped at her coffee. "Have a seat, Zemuel."

He narrowed his eyes at her. "Sophia DeMonstre? I haven't seen you since you were a teen."

"I know, but you make an impression."

When he sat, the chair creaked. For beings that flew, dragons were not lightweights. He picked up the cup of coffee that Minerva had left behind. He flicked his tongue out a disturbing—or intriguing—degree and scowled. "I missed her by minutes."

"You did. She was out of here like a scalded cat. So, why are you stalking her?"

He flicked his bat-like wings and smiled. "She's mine. She's perfect and she is mine."

He was elegantly dressed, as always. Dragons had an innate fashion sense. His dark shirt set off his silver skin and dark-grey hair. He was a man made of stone and air. It was a strange combination, but it suited him.

"I know that you think so, but she is her own being first. Remember that when you deal with her. She is also powerful enough to take any appendages you have and turn them into innies."

He smirked. "I will keep it in mind. How goes your hunt for a mate?"

"I have only started."

"What about that mage?"

"Alaneus? He is after my pedigree. I need someone who can be a partner."

"Ah, interesting. That is a tall order. Your family has grown more powerful with every generation."

She smiled, "We aren't up to dragon standard, but we do all right."

She paused as she realized that it meant Minerva *was* powerful enough to attract a dragon. Well, it made sense. She was the most impressive mage that Sophy had ever met.

"I might start looking in the elves. They usually go after blondes with weirdly long lifespans and consistent youth."

"Invite me to the nuptials. I would like to see what you consider to be a good match."

She raised her bowl to him. "Keep me posted if you catch Minerva. She's a quick one."

He sighed. "I know. Her trail is gone now. She knew I was coming."

"There's a seer here. So, yeah, she

knew.”

He grimaced, his fine silver features pulling for a moment before they smoothed into incorruptible planes again. He looked carved of silver and was very pretty to watch.

Jennifer and Magnus were still in detailed discussion about whatever Jennifer was seeing. When the cup shattered in her hands, she looked over to Sophy with wild eyes.

“I believe that is my cue to leave. I do apologize, Zemuel. All the ladies seem to be running out on you tonight.”

“My ego can take it. Have a good night, Sophia.” He reached out and kissed the back of her hand.

She blinked and smiled. “That never gets old.”

“Good to know. Nice to know I still have moves.” He winked and inclined his head.

She glanced to Magnus, but he was

already on his feet. She left the café and headed for her car. He was right behind her.

They headed back to her house, and she said something before she could change her mind. "You can sleep in my bed until we find something else."

He nodded. "That is very agreeable."

She thought about what she would need to kit out the couch, but there was no way he would fit, so it had to be her.

Chapter Eleven

Sophy was grinning when she woke up. Magnus had been pissed when he realized she wasn't sharing the bed. Taking the couch was uncomfortable, but it was better than snuggling up to someone who had no interest in her.

She tiptoed through the bedroom and into her bathroom. She brushed her teeth and took a quick shower before she clued into her lack of clean clothing. Magic in her home was limited, so she crept back into the bedroom, wearing a towel and water.

"You can feel free to drop the towel. Your virtue is safe with me."

She stiffened but flicked on the light

from across the room. "Sorry. I didn't mean to wake you."

"I wasn't sleeping. I have spent centuries asleep. I was thinking about what you said."

She collected her underwear and a tunic and leggings.

"You can tell me about that when I have changed."

She slipped into the bathroom again and changed with as much speed as she could manage. She entered the bedroom again and wished she hadn't.

Clothed, Magnus was impressive. Naked, he was the perfection of a statue come to life. Hairier but still perfect.

He stretched and she stared. Finally, she shook herself and left without saying a word. She made her own coffee and waited while the drips cascaded through the machine.

Delwin woke up and greeted her before pulling out a griddle that she didn't know she had and starting pancakes.

Magnus came out wearing only the jeans from the day before. "I believe I am going to need to work on my wardrobe."

She took at the hair on his chest, the muscles and the pattern of scars, and she nodded absently. "Yeah."

Delwin smiled. "If I didn't know you slept on the couch, I would say you have morning-after fascination, Sophia."

With Magnus grinning at her fixation, she blushed and fixed her coffee. "Right. I will be back in one piece or blown to hell and back. 'scuse me."

"What about pancakes?" Delwin whined.

"Put them under the warmer, and I will be back in a moment. I just need to finish another phase of the process."

She escaped. There was no other word for it. She sprinted to the workshop and locked the door behind her.

With deliberate focus and a cup of coffee fuelling her, she set the solutions to distill and returned to the house.

The pancakes were ready, and she took a stack of three, pouring syrup on them before topping them with a cube of butter. Bacon would have been perfect, but beggars couldn't be choosers.

The boys were somewhere else. She ate in silence, got a second helping and ate that as well. After, she put her dishes in the washer and headed back to the workshop with a fresh cup of coffee.

She fiddled with the distillers and checked the level of final product. Another hour and it would be enough.

"How is it coming?" Magnus asked her from the doorway.

"Almost ready."

"So, I would like to straighten out a few things from yesterday."

She glanced at him. "It isn't necessary."

"Yes, it is. You do not have final say on this. I do find you attractive; I have just been working with you for a week and am interested in you achieving your goals. Your current goal is to remove that curse, and that is what I have been focusing on. I saw the problem; I didn't see you. That was my mistake, and I apologize."

She inclined her head. "I accept your apology, but I still have work to do."

"And I am here to assist you, but afterward, I would like to pursue you."

The phrasing was weird, but she smiled. "Fine. Let's get through this, and then, we will see what is what."

"Right. What can I do?"

She smiled. "Turn up that flame and watch for ten millilitres of liquid in the receptacle."

He did as she asked, and together, they accelerated the condensation process until they had what was needed.

They shut down the flames, and she looked at the small quantities of blue and red liquid.

She set a third beaker down and got the book out of the secure cabinet.

She loaded everything on a tray and carried it into what she termed the *exercise room*. If anything was going to be blown up, this was the place to do it.

The worktable in the middle of the room was wood and bolted to the floor. She set the tray down and took a few deep breaths.

"Magnus, you might want to wait outside."

He shook his head and closed the door, bolting it. "No, I need to be here for this."

She thought he just wanted to observe. She placed her hands on the case and started to chant in harsh words that scraped her throat. The two liquids on either side of the book began to boil, and the case bucked.

Sophia felt the heat under her hands and let go of the book, grabbing the two liquids, dumping them into the empty third container and then grabbing it and doing a shot of scalding magical concentrate.

She focused and sprayed the case with a fine mist of the liquid. Across the magical plain, she could feel the layers of spell work crack until they broke apart.

She finished spraying the charmed liquid over the case and resumed her pressure to break the curse on the object.

Instead of losing power, the surge of energy knocked her backward. The backwash of power hurt every inch of her, and she screamed as she was pushed to the wall.

The power poured out for an eternity until it suddenly stopped.

Laughter rang through the room, and it wasn't pleasant laughter.

She opened her eyes and saw the face from the book of demons.

"Arion."

He smiled and stepped toward her, his rams horns curling wildly on his head. "Ah, the Cursed One. I have to admit that I didn't think you would be able to do it, but you did. You pulled me from the demon zone and into the human world again. How delightful."

He stepped toward her, grabbing her by the front of her tunic and pulling her up against the wall. "What a pretty little thing you are. I have my freedom and a pet, all in one."

A low growl came from the side of the room. "Put her down, Father."

Dazed, Sophia looked over toward Magnus.

He was standing tall, his dark hair flowing down his back, shoulders wide, and two long spiralling horns emerged from his forehead.

"You are one of mine? How delightful. Give me a moment while I break her in and you can have a turn." Arion licked down her neck and over the front of her tunic.

Her senses were screaming so loudly she was deafened. This was a true monster, and she was acting as bait whether she intended to or not.

Magnus was a foot shorter than Arion, but he still managed to spin the demon around.

Sophia dropped to the floor, and she landed hard but got herself together. She couldn't use defensive spells, but she could use protective spells for someone else. She concentrated on Magnus as he attacked with fists and horns.

The wounds that the demon inflicted were healed seconds later, and Magnus was goring and slashing at Arion with fury. He was getting stronger with every step.

She focused on him and pushed herself to dump as much power into Magnus as she could manage. His skin turned the same glossy pearl as his horns, and Arion's attacks skidded off his skin.

The demon fell back and dropped to his knees. Finally, he began to beg for relief.

Magnus growled. "You should not have touched her."

He reached up, cracked off one horn and ran it through Arion's chest.

Sophia had never seen a demon die before. The light went from his eyes, and the power in his body flared outward in a cataclysmic explosion that flung her back once again.

She woke up being carried out of the workshop. "What happened?"

Magnus was looking like himself again. "You managed to remove the curse on the flute case."

She smiled and leaned against his chest. "Oh good. I think it gave me a hallucination. Shit got weird."

Magnus pressed a kiss to her temple. "Yes, it did. I am surprised you aren't complaining about me being a quarter demon."

"Oh. That. That was real?"

He was carrying her into the house and heading for her bedroom.

He set her down in her bed and smoothed his hand over her head. "Yes, it was real."

She smiled and touched her head. "I think I got a concussion."

"Likely. You hit the wall a few times."

She blinked. "That was real?"

"Yes. I think I should use a healing charm on you while I tell you the story of my family."

She looked up at him. "You are going to tell me a story?"

He shook his head with a smile. "Yes, I am."

He lifted her up again, turned and sat on her bed, propping himself against the headboard before he began to tell her about his family. She was settled across his lap.

"I come from a long line of unicorns. Nine generations were all unicorn shifters. Each member found their match and donated their horns as necessary for healing spells."

He hugged her. "My mother told me that she was on her way to heal some locals when Arion appeared in front of her. What followed was short and violent, but he couldn't keep her because of her nature, and the demon blood became the recessive gene. She got away, and I was the result."

"You look human. Your aura registers

as that of a mage."

He chuckled. "Yes, it does. That is how I was able to be in the guild for hundreds of years before I faced off against Arion in a public place. I managed to wound him but exposed myself in the process. That is what instigated my time in amber."

"You got taller and you have horns."

"Yes. I only need that form to fight."

She looked up at him. She pressed her hand to his cheek. "Still not a monster."

He blinked rapidly. "That is not what the guild thinks."

"They aren't cursed to know a monster when they see it. You are not a monster."

He held her and smiled. "I can heal the rest of your damage if you will let me."

She nodded. "That would be for the best. I think I cracked my skull, and I am not up to calling my parents."

Magnus smiled, and he got bigger. His thighs widened, his shoulders grew broader, his fingernails became thick claws, and the horns sprouted from his forehead.

"You broke a horn off."

His voice was deeper when he said, "It regenerates for every transformation. It is unbreakable for anyone but me."

She watched as he bent his head to her, his horns gently resting against her skull. A wash of cool energy ran over her skin like melted snow.

She breathed deep and relaxed against him as the energy crept under her skin and fixed all of her cracks, bumps and bruises.

"Do you often get battered like this on your missions?" He stroked her cheek softly.

"More often than not. Most monsters don't come quietly, and Arion was definitely a monster. Is there any of him left?"

"No, he shattered, and the energy returned through the vortex to the demon zone. Orbithon might come after you one day, but Arion is over."

"Good. Is it safe for me to sleep now?"

"Sleep. I will watch over you."

She nodded and let the fatigue of the day go, embracing healing sleep.

Delwin walked in with a cup of tea, saw Magnus's shifted shape cradling Sophia as if she was fine porcelain and slowly backed out. They were working out their relationship, and if this kind of trust was the start, he wasn't going to interrupt them.

He snuck back into the kitchen and picked up the phone. He dialled quickly, and when the familiar voice answered, he whispered, "There has been some progress. She's trusting him."

Lillian DeMonstre smiled into her phone. "Excellent. Keep me posted as to progress."

"This is a little odd, ma'am."

"I know, but she can't back up now. I don't want her putting barriers between herself and possible happiness. He is the best candidate I have found. Keep me informed, Delwin, and I will keep your grandmother at bay."

"Yes, ma'am."

The phone went silent, and Lillian let out a long sigh. Two years of negotiations and machinations had finally given her daughter a chance at a partner and, hopefully, a husband.

The biggest hurdle was Magnus's own

nature. The unicorn in him was attract-ed to purity, but the demon in him was repelled by it. He tended to lock up around virgins.

Lillian didn't know what had hap-pened, but somehow, they both had to push past their inclinations and find each other. If they were in the trust phase, they would be lovers soon.

Lillian looked over to where her hus-band was cheerfully talking with a client. She wanted a grandchild so she could enjoy her daughter again. Her daughter hadn't been hers for twenty years, and it made her heart ache that her little girl had to go out there and face perverse danger night after night. Now, finally, there was a chance she wouldn't have to continue on alone.

Chapter Twelve

She opened her eyes and was confronted by Magnus, his face only inches from hers. "Why do you wear long tunics?"

Sophia thought about the answer and settled for, "I have to wear so many costumes that I like to just be myself when I can. The tunic is the most basic form of clothing available, and I like it. It is shapeless and comfy."

"You don't like advertising your body."

She wrinkled her nose. "That is another way of saying it."

He stroked her cheek. "You are lovely no matter what you wear."

She blushed. "Thanks for that."

"I spent a week as your electronics; I have seen you from every angle. You are kind to those who are hurt and confused, and practical when there is a job to be done. That doesn't just come from training; it comes from your soul."

She was already blushing an inch from him. There was nowhere to go. "Thanks for that... again."

He chuckled and pulled her in for a hug. They were lying face to face on her bed, and her clothing had been removed. He was naked as well. She stiffened up at the impact of all that hard skin, and he stroked his hand over her spine. Her relaxation came in tiny increments, but he didn't seem to be in a hurry.

"You have seen my nature. Do you understand why I did not lunge for you the moment that I saw you?"

She nodded; her nose rubbed the crook of his neck. "I understand. Attraction and repulsion in equal measure become a static state.”

“Of course you would understand. Well, attraction is winning, and the repulsion died with Arion.”

“Gee. I feel so special.”

He chuckled. “You know the constraints of magic and the nature of beasts.”

“I do. I just hate to be on the receiving end of that kind of attitude. Just because you understand something doesn’t mean you like it.”

Magnus continued to stroke her back. “I will make you a deal. I will be your partner when you go out as the Cursed One, and you will have dinner with me once a week. Oh, and we will share the bed.”

She frowned. “That is a lot of demands. What do I get out of it?”

“One of the greatest mages of the ages and a companion who understands your nature as well as you do."

Sophia looked up at him. "You are serious?"

"I am. I will prove that I am the best candidate to be your mate, and I will do it by the effect of proximity."

She was quiet for a moment and then asked, "How many other bicorns are their out there?"

He chuckled. "As far as my mother has been able to tell, I am the only one."

"And you were slutty enough that you couldn't find a woman you hadn't slept with to ask for your freedom?"

He rubbed his chin on her head. "I was following my baser instinct and that led me to the married ladies of the Mage Guild. When an irate husband caught me, it spurred on my transformation and the amber came next."

"So, you were punished for being promiscuous more than for being a creature."

"The Archmage certainly wanted to kill me, and he did try, but it was thought that the amber would leave the building standing."

"And you went quietly."

"I hadn't aged up until then. I could wait for the chance to come out and look for a proper mate, fighting my instincts the whole way."

"Why was it a concern? Why want a family? And why did you need a mate to do it?"

"That is the unicorn part of me. I want children, always have. The mix of chaos in my loins kept me from procreating. That is why my mother encouraged the guild to put me in amber. It would give me time to balance myself out. It did. When they came to me, I was more than ready to serve you in any capacity. My time with you gave me a respect for your thoroughness and intellect. My body was just the last to follow the path."

She burrowed into his embrace, pulling herself tight to him. "Remind me to tell you of the first Cursed One. She had a pen pal that turned into her partner, and they founded our dynasty, such as it is."

"I think I would like that story, but now, Delwin has made dinner, so we need to get you up and fed."

She reached up and stroked his forehead. "The horns are very pretty when they are there."

"You don't mind the monstrous look?"

She chuckled. "I keep telling you. I know what a monster looks like, and you are not it."

Eventually, they stopped cuddling long enough to get up and have part of the meatloaf casserole that Delwin had created. He hadn't skimped on the cheese, and it was appreciated.

Epilogue

Lillian settled on her chair in the Patchwork Dragon. The chai blend was aromatic, and the milk gave it the appearance of the mist over the mountains.

Her companion arrived with all the grace and elegance of her kind. A double shot latte with chocolate sprinkles was her potion of choice.

They sat and sipped at their drinks for a minute, and then, Elsinor smiled. "Thank you for the idea. I never imagined that he would go after your daughter. She is so very superficially pretty."

Lillian inclined her head. "Thank you. As your son has all the grace and charm of an ancient barbarian, it will be a good match. She pulls out his intelligence, and he reminds her that she is more than her curse."

Elsinor cocked her head. "It has been two months, and she is still a virgin."

Lillian quirked her lips. "If you say so. I believe they are becoming familiar with each other before finally completing the cycle. They are not in a hurry, so we should not be in a hurry."

Elsinor scowled. "I want a grand-child."

"Don't lose your serene aura, your horny highness." Lillian sipped at her cup.

She had met the unicorn in school, as her student. As time passed, they realized they had points of commonality and that included their desire to see a better future for magic. When Lillian married a DeMonstre and became the female companion to the Cursed One, it gave her a different perspective than had been held before. She wanted to choose the best guardian for her own daughter, and for decades, it had been Sophia herself.

If Sophia had to have a partner, he had to be strong, smart, witty, and the fact that he could still take over technology to spy was a very handy feature in a Cursed One's companion.

"I told you about my nature in confidence."

Lillian waved it away. "In modern vernacular, it just means that you seek out sexual companionship."

Elsinor's elegant hair was curled befitting a 1950s' heroine in a spy novel. When she frowned, it was the cutest pout. She couldn't help being herself, even if she had once been touched by evil.

"I don't know what will become of them if they continue this slow waltz toward sex. Someone might get in between them and block their attentions."

Lillian blinked. "You really haven't seen them together. You can't even get a sheet of tissue paper between them. Their pace is their own. We just have to wait for the final result."

"I want the girl named for my side of the family."

Lillian chuckled. "If the Cursed One is a girl, it will be named after her side of the family. Your name will be second. If it is a boy, we can call him Elsinor all day long."

Elsinor scowled. "Arm wrestle you for it."

Jennifer looked over and watched the two beautiful women square off and battle over the name of a child that hadn't even become reality.

Jennifer smiled at the images that overlaid the women. One had a tremendous mane of hair and a solid horn; the other was made of coursing flame and power. It was a pretty fair fight.

Of course, Jennifer already knew the name of the little one that would arrive in just over a year. The little girl would buck convention in every sense. Her several sisters would also throw a wrench into the DeMonstre works as they went from one Cursed One to a small squad that could reach farther and work together.

The next generation was definitely going to mix things up, but the first baby was still going to be named—

She turned toward the server touching her elbow. "What?"

"Jennifer, table three wants a reading."

Jennifer smiled and headed for table

three. Her life might have been changed by magic, but for her, it was for the better.

For Sophia, things were just about to get very interesting. Her mom was one tough mage.

Author's Note

That's right. Another one with no sex. Fortunately, *Binding Magic* will have it. It is already built in.

Sophia needed a bit of a transformation from monster hunter into fiancé. It took some doing, but I think I got her there.

Thanks for reading. I hope to have *Binding Magic* out in 6 weeks or so. Hopefully sooner.

Viola Grace

About the Author

Viola Grace (aka Zenina Masters) is a Canadian sci-fi/paranormal romance writer with ambitions to keep writing for the rest of her life. She specializes in short stories because the thrill of discovery, of all those firsts, is what keeps her writing.

An artist who enjoys a story that catches you up, whirls you around and sets you down with a smile on your face is all she endeavours to be. She prefers to leave the drama to those who are better suited to it, she always goes for the cheap laugh.